Marla-Tiye Vieira is also the fiction author of *Jasmine Breeze*. Vieira viscerally combats racism, homophobia and religious oppression throughout her writing in order to create world peace. She holds a bachelor's degree in Broadcast Journalism and French from Howard University and a master's degree in Second Language Education and Curriculum & Instruction from the University of Houston.

Vieira has an immense passion for wildlife and is a devoted advocate for Earth conservation. During her third trip to South Africa, she witnessed two great white sharks for a second time and dove with Nile crocodiles in Gansbaai. In South Africa, she earned a Volunteer Certificate in June of 2023 with *White Shark Projects*.

Lastly, her most spiritual emprise was her third excursion to Australia in March of 2024 where she snorkeled and dove with four whale sharks in Ningaloo Reef, a UNESCO world heritage site.

To my dad, Myers Allen Evans, who was my superhero during my entire childhood. He recently transitioned on June 27, 2023 to join my magnanimous mother: Ada D. Evans inside this mystical realm. He taught me how to do one of my favorite pastimes: ride a bicycle. I vividly remember when I had my training wheels removed, and how he guided me until I rode independently. While racing forward, I turned around and realized that he was no longer holding on to my seat. He was way in the distance. I was so afraid. In spite of my trepidation, I was free to fly on my bike, which I do on a daily basis 50 years later. Love you, Dad! Thanks for instilling freedom within me!

Marla-Tiye Vieira

CHERRY BLOSSOM BLUES

AUSTIN MACAULEY PUBLISHERS™

LONDON • CAMBRIDGE • NEW YORK • SHARJAH

Ordering Information
Quantity sales: Special discounts are available on quantity purchases by corporations, associations, and others. For details, contact the publisher at the address below.

Publisher's Cataloging-in-Publication data
Vieira, Marla-Tiye
Cherry Blossom Blues

ISBN 9798891550070 (Paperback)
ISBN 9798891550087 (Hardback)
ISBN 9798891550094 (ePub e-book)

Library of Congress Control Number: 2023920986

www.austinmacauley.com/us

First Published 2024
Austin Macauley Publishers LLC
40 Wall Street, 33rd Floor, Suite 3302
New York, NY 10005
USA

mail-usa@austinmacauley.com
+1 (646) 5125767

I first want to thank Benji for being my constant muse! In addition, I amply appreciate my bonny brother's generous financial contribution from our late father's estate. Also, Stacey Grod of Central Library in Cape Town, South Africa, for allowing me to empower our youth via my second Author Talk for my first novella, *'Jasmine Breeze'*. A huge thank you also goes to Brianna Eusebio of Mesa Public Library in Arizona for permitting me to conduct my first Author Talk. Additionally, I want to express my gratitude to fellow writer and Opera Star: Sophia Grech for her continued support. I am ever grateful to Reverend 'Ems' McGowan who provided my first author podcast. I must also thank Mesa Community College via the Mesa Legend Newspaper, Howard University Magazine, University of Houston's Alumni Library, the Press of Atlantic City, Tom Maxedon, Barnes & Noble of Chandler, Arizona, both Chandler and Scottsdale public libraries of Arizona, Mikako Murakami, White Shark Projects, Ahwatukee Foothills News, Xplorio Gansbaai, *She Blurbs*, as well as the *Arizona Informant Newspaper* for their incessant encouragement of my authorship.

Table of Contents

Author's Note

Transcending our egos is pivotal to communing and actualizing with divinity. My aim is always to create world peace by examining the ludicrousness of our human condition by revealing this explicit aspect to the masses. Humans are such complex and innovative beings, yet our dichotomy lies in our deep delusion. Very few people experientially know that we are an integral part of a dynamic and eternal cosmos. Compared to our vast universe, we are just an infinitesimal component of an immeasurable and awe-inspiring realm of this massive and primordial innovation. No codification needed because the National Aeronautics and Space Administration (NASA) recently shared its images using the James Webb space telescope evincing a mirror of ourselves dating back to 4.6 billion years ago. We are the microcosm of the macrocosmic cosmos. Our spiritual transcendence is depicted as the visual universe. Separation is Maya, or illusion. While most of us are imprisoned by our limited identities: race, gender, polity, religion, sexual orientations and socioeconomic delineations, truth and limitless prosperity are always awaiting us. Thus, the enslaved cannot perceive our enduring interconnections with totality.

Consciously, we must realize how to break the shackles of misconceptions that keep us in isolation, misery and confusion. I dedicate this work to two great healers and teachers: Sadhguru and Dr. Michael Bernard Beckwith during this epic epoque of a monumental purge of humanity. They profess authentic liberation and spiritual freedom by edifying us on how to see and elicit our true nature. Dolefully, so many of us are ignorantly motivated by external forces that incessantly disconnect us from infinity and all things tangible.

Our species is responsible for global warming, which is wreaking havoc on our planet. Earth is a living and dynamic organism, not just some dead rock where we reside. When we hurt her, we inevitably harm ourselves and all organisms that dwell here. Perceived separation is the travesty that is destroying us. Regrettably, we are probably the only species responsible for causing the onset of this current mass 6th extinction on Earth. Previous mass extinctions were triggered by outside factors like asteroids or rampant volcanism. Consuming meat, producing fossil fuels, the threat of nuclear war, deforestation, mining for minerals, and polluting our air and oceans are slowly obliterating our only home. Not to mention the incessant barrage of mass shootings throughout these recent years, killing and maiming innocent mortals whilst providing minimum gun protections, and the lack of legal ramifications from the National Rifle Association of America (NRA). White cancer cells and Covid 19 cannot be detected with the naked eye, but they have the capability to take life from us swiftly and effortlessly. Most human behavior emulates cancer and deadly viruses within our bodies with the same repercussions because we are making our planet Earth gravely sick. On a positive note, a brilliant breakthrough from our species has finally come into fruition. We now know how to harness star energy, or nuclear fusion…the essential essence of our sun. Nuclear fusion can save our Earth by using clean energy, so she can rebuild and repair herself without us resorting to fossil fuels anymore.

Most indigenous people honor and respect our planet because they possess the deep insights that we are intrinsically intertwined together as one body. The terminology 'separation' does not exist in their mindsets. Even death is a phase of transitioning to another dimension that can be accessed by the living and vice versa. Each paradigm and dimension serve different purposes for various events. These phases exist to propel souls to familiarize ourselves with the essence of eternity. All religions offer different modalities to reach the same goal: wholeness. My intent is unific consciousness. Because God created everything, I am wise enough to know that I am unable to conceptualize what God is. However, I feel oneness with our universe which emanates from inside myself because we are connected to eternity. Empirically, I have faith in knowing that there is a divine order and presence regulating our cosmos. Again, we are a microcosm of a macrocosmic spiritual system. I espouse spirituality, where I see God (our creator) in everything. I had to evolve to reach this particular viewpoint. My faith in the universe is antrorsely great. In spite of all of the hideousness that occurs on Earth, I know that there is a grand purpose because we are connected to something so much bigger than ourselves. I deem that the key to obtaining true love is to exude equanimity. It is an arduous task, but it can be accomplished. I was born and raised a Christian and fervently followed this pious epistemology until I was 18 years old. However, during my freshman year at Howard University, this concept drastically metamorphosed within myself. Their names escape me now, but their profound pedagogies promulgate within me forever. Felicitously, I had two political science professors: a female from New York City and a male from the Caribbean islands who did a brilliant job of delineating colonization and the root causes of White Supremacy. To my dismay, these professors taught that Christianity was instrumentally utilized to murder, enslave and indoctrinate the African diaspora and indigenous people worldwide and continues to brainwash and instill self-hatred and self-deprivation. Since that time, I divorced myself from the church or any form of organized religion because this newfound knowledge draped my consciousness like a baleful betrayal. I have been bamboozled! Upon further investigation, I was edified to uncover the Papal movement where Pope Nicholas V commissioned European colonizers to subjugate and impose White Supremacist ideologies upon indigenous and non-Christian nations worldwide. Papal supremacy preempts White supremacy more than 500 years ago. Hence, the Vatican ordained slavery, carnage and the allowance of stolen lands from People of Color throughout the Americas. Sadly, most people use religion as a tool for separation, as opposed to planetary unification which it is designed to do. Too many homosexuals are demonized by their respective religions. Hence, they are dying to conform to a creed of oppression by limiting their human expression.

I deem that churches, temples and other places of worship must embrace its members equally regardless of their backgrounds and not espouse one culture over another. Amazingly, these self-righteous institutions proport misogyny. Thus, women are still trying to find equal ground amongst many societal norms today. Furthermore, these religious institutions should promote preserving nature as a pivotal priority, as opposed to acquiring money. So many human beings are asleep and need to be awake in order to know contentment and liberation. Yes, I am a prolific proponent of the "Woke Movement." Obtaining these states of deliverance can be very painful and frightening because it is like entering an unknown abyss. For example, when a fetus is released from his or her mother's warm womb inhaling liquids through our lungs for nine months in complete darkness, this tremendous transitioning into a brightly lit portal forces us to learn how to breathe a foreign substance: air. Infants scream to the top of our lungs when the death of the womb happens and our rebirth into the light manifests. Yes, sometimes we must let go of familiarities which no longer serve us because familiarities often breed ferities. I will always value my freedom and I refuse to cajole anyone by diminishing my brilliance and not letting my light shine. Seeking freedom can be a terrifying and an unsettling stunt like diving deep into an oceanic unknown abysm. However, the underwater treasures that I have discovered by being true to myself and stepping out on faith are priceless.

Like my first novella, 'Jasmine Breeze', I continue to use flowers and music as my central themes to disseminate the plots, settings and characterization via my writings.

Flowers due to their prolific proliferations are the most sexual organisms on our planet. Their scents and physical designs are always beckoning other creatures to help them procreate. Music is a universal medium that conjures scents, moments in time: past and present and potential inspirations. Hence, music transports us to a cornucopia of realms. My aim is to have this second novella be another vindication for oppressed groups living under various subjugated regimes. Unlike, *Jasmine Breeze,* death is the central motif of *Cherry Blossom Blues.* I choose cherry blossoms from Japan because they symbolize impermanence. The Japanese word for cherry blossom is Sakura. In Japan, cherry blossoms represent the impermanent nature of life because their petals' lifespan is extremely brief. Cherry blossoms symbolize both birth and death because their petals peak around two weeks. They are harbingers of change and the quintessential symbols of life and death. After this timeframe, they perish and gravity grounds them. As a cosmic family, once we recognize this omnipresent impermanence, we will embark on a trajectory of positivity that will multiply incrementally. The following Buddhist tenet encapsulates 'Cherry Blossom Blues' by recently departed Thich Nhat Hanh. "This body is not me; I am not caught in this body, I am life without boundaries, I have never been born and I have never died. Over there the wide ocean and the sky with many galaxies All manifests from the basis of consciousness. Since beginningless time, I have always been free. Birth and death are only a door through which we go in and out. Birth and death are only a game of hide-and-seek. So smile to me and take my hand and wave goodbye. Tomorrow we shall meet again or even before. We shall always be meeting again at the true source, Always meeting again on the myriad paths of life."

With the recent passing of Great Britain's Queen Elizabeth II, it is mindboggling to perceive that her biracial grandchildren belong to the top-tier of the British Royal family and they could possibly inherit the throne because of the marriage between Prince Harry, the Duke of Sussex and the biracial (Afro-American and European American) bride, Meghan, the Duchess of Sussex. Wow, Meghan now belongs to the highest echelon of European society: the British Monarchy! King Charles III of the United Kingdom is the father-in-law of a half-black commoner/actress from Los Angeles, California. Let's address the elephant in the room. Since colorism, the issue of passing Blacks and their privileges are major themes associated in 'Cherry Blossom Blues', it is very contemporaneous with the current reality that many people around the world are either exceedingly curious to know and/or have intense angst on how ethnic or Negroid these royal babies: Lilibett Diana and Archie Harrison will look as they grow older...wink, wink. The adage that 'The empire on which the sun never sets' is slowly fading away because England now has its first East Indian prime minister: Rishi Sunak, who was born and raised in East Africa.

Evermore, I deem that the key to obtaining true love is to transcend our egos. It is an arduous task, but it can be accomplished because this is the segue to unifying with eternity. I encourage my readership to supplement their understanding of *Cherry Blossom Blues* by reading *The Wretched of the Earth* by Frantz Fanon and *Pedagogy of the Oppressed* by Paulo Freire in order to enable us to consciously break the shackles of mental delusion, spiritual dissolution and denigration. Moreover, I also recommend my novella to those who suffer from a pretense of superiority. I am going to continue to fight the good fight until racism, homophobia and religious intolerance no longer exist because everyone deserves the unalienable right to be free and content. I must confess that I am still grieving my mother's death going on six years. So, this book is very cathartic for me. Speaking of death, my father, Myers Allen Evans, died two weeks later, shortly after my return trip from Cape Town, South Africa for a third time during Pride Month. His unpredictable demise blind sighted me, but I am blessed to have celebrated his last Father's Day with him in 2023.

I am a film buff and one of my favorite movies is 'K-PAX'. The protagonist, Prot sagaciously stipulates how our universe functions in relation to everything, assuming that our species is unaware of this fact. Prot posits, "The universe will expand, then it will collapse back on itself, then will expand again. It will repeat this process forever. What you don't know is that when the universe expands again, everything will be as it is now. Whatever mistakes you make this time around, you will live through on your next pass." My aim is to show how precious and short life really is. Try to forgive and leave pettiness, jealousy, and hostility in the refuse where it belongs. Please know that there is a universal law already put in place that accounts for and balances all acts in an equanimous way, so we don't have to do anything, but just be, as blissful as can be.

As tenuous as times are, this is nothing new under the sun. History repeats because we are in a cultural war, and banning books by people of color that address historical atrocities perpetrated by White Supremacists are at the forefront in today's society. The old guard is trying to suppress truth by obstructing critical race theory. The guise to protect and coddle the sentiments of descendants of White Supremacy is so disingenuous because the authentic mission is to continue promoting White supremacist ideologies, even though it is a dying creed worldwide. White supremacists are obsessed solely with power; they will resort to any violent schemes to attain it. Russian President Vladimir Vladimirovich Putin is a fascist leader attempting to murder Jewish President Volodymyr Oleksandrovych Zelenskyy of Ukraine. Putin is the last bastion of a White supremacist regime with fervent supporters around the world. The Russian Imperial Movement (RIM) is an Evangelical White Supremacist group supporting the demolition of Ukraine and they militarily train Neo-Nazis around the world to usurp republics wherever they live. The United States has labeled them as a terrorist group. Speaking of Putin's loyalists, nine years before Trump's Mar-a-Lago fiasco of leaking classified U.S. documents to foreign and rogue governments, in 2013 another former government employee: Edward Snowden who was a computer intelligence consultant with the National Security Agency, also illegally sent highly classified U.S. information to Russia and other enemies of the state. Snowden's cowardice behavior to evade criminal conviction influenced him to flee and defect to Russia nine years ago. This villainous Russian supporter and subversive mole: Snowden is now a Russian citizen. As opposed to having dual citizenship,

Snowden belongs under a U.S. prison with the key thrown away for the rest of his life for his insurrectionist and treasonous acts. Putin's last resort is to threaten to decimate our entire planet via nuclear weapons. Also, on August 4, 2022, the Hungarian autocratic prime minister, Viktor Orbán, professed his delusory tenets of Christianity under the guise of White nationalism, or neo-Nazism, at the Conservative Political Action Conference (CPAC) with Donald Trump and other extreme right-wing radicals in Dallas, Texas. He rudely and blatantly snubbed President Joseph Robinette Biden's White House administration in order to disseminate his anti-Lesbian, Gay, Bisexual, Transgender and Questioning (LGBTQ) views and racialist rhetoric of separation and denigration, as the Santa Ana winds willfully fuel deadly forest fires. Fascist manifestation cascades heavily throughout the United States due to the rise of domestic terrorism and the malignant mayhem thrust upon law enforcement. The single-minded goal of fascists around the world is to implement and enforce a Christian White ethnostate. Germany is not immune from this same affliction due to the recent arrests of over 25 organizers within the Reichsbürger movement. The Reichsbürger movement includes teachers, judges, and politicians, as old as 71 years. Everyone should know that the mayhem in Europe stemming from Nazi Germany during World War II was a playbook stolen from the United States of America. America's roots are dredged in bloody anti-Semitism. To not live in truth plummets one to stifle in total darkness. Some people never learn! September 11th has two notorious dates, one in particular during 1973 when Augusto Pinochet seized power in Chile via a coup d'état. Pinochet established his dictatorship after he overthrew the democratic government of Salvador Allende. Why is Pinochet internationally chastised for his egregious treatment of fellow Chileans? Benito Mussolini could not even successfully colonize Ethiopia via fascism. Furthermore, he led Italy into a global war and stifling recession. In spite of this fact and almost 100 years later, Giorgia Meloni, is elected as the first female fascist prime minister with an overwhelming win in Italy. How did World War II end for the Nazis? Did these militarized miscreants fare well throughout Europe decades following the Second World War? Was this particular regime that plummeted from a democracy to a dictatorship successful? The genocide and decimation of more than six million Jews should never, ever happen again! We should always be on the right side of history, as opposed to being idle and complicit bystanders. One of the greatest scientific minds ever to inhabit our planet happens to be of the Jewry diaspora. Albert Einstein coined derangement best with the following utterance: "Insanity is doing the same thing over and over and expecting different results." The U.S. has been a beacon of hope for over 200 years for countries around the world. Losing our democracy would dishearten billions of people and leave them with an overwhelming feeling of hopelessness.

Societal obstructions prevail via the recent book bans based on extolling truth regarding European Colonization of indigenous people worldwide and its drastic effects resonating to this present moment. Additionally, the latest legislation put in place in many states and countries proscribes the freedoms of our (LGBTQ) Communities.

Misogyny still exists in the U.S. as women's reproductive rights are legally under attack. Just like our guiltless female predecessors during the Salem Witch trials, the United States continues to burn us alive at the stake because we have the gall to be free, independent and strong. Thus, the U.S. Supreme Court upended Roe versus Wade after 50 years of legality! Exactly one year to the date, this same court also annihilates Affirmative Action as a vetting criterion to ensure that racial diversity is preserved within colleges and universities via student matriculation. To make matters worse…the following day, this sham of a Supreme court denies Student Debt Cancellation, which is a brilliant proposal by President Biden to assuage economic hardships for millions of collegiate learners residing within the United States, including myself. Just when we think that matters cannot get any worse, this despicable court ruled in favor of a Christian web designer who refuses to honor and acknowledge same-sex weddings. I will always label myself as a fiction writer who combats racism, homophobia and religious oppression. The U.S. Supreme Court has proven that my fight is more important now, then ever.

Most appalling is the blasphemous depiction and deliberate targeting of journalists for bestowing objectivity. I would be remiss if I omit the vast campaign for voter suppression disseminated under the guise of averting corrupt elections within fascists nations whenever White supremacists loose elections. Some of us are moving backwards, which is sorely self-defeating. Alternatively, we should progress and propel ourselves towards a forward trajectory.

An octillion kudos to these magnanimous defenders of democracy, such as Antifa and the Red Neck Revolt, better known as the 'John Brown Gun Club' because they help to keep a defensive equilibrium among offensive far-right fascist groups. They are our true liberators within society because we (USA) are on the precipice of having our second Civil War. Thus, Antifa and the John Brown Gun Club are dedicated dismantlers of White Supremacy who incessantly and unapologetically demand equality for all, instead of White, Anglo-Saxon, wealthy, Protestant, rich men. Most importantly, their valiant efforts could secure and preserve American democracy, which is in deep peril.

The grave lack of civility in polity within the United States is pestilential dissemination by the Maga movement, or shall I call them mega miscreants? Anywho, when MAGA loyalists think that it is okay to break into democratic offices and homes to steal vital information and murder leftist politicians, they are leading a very delusional and psychotic existence. Luckily, Secretary of State, Katie Hobbs of Arizona was not present when her invader raided her office. However, Paul Pelosi was not as fortunate. He is an 80-year old man who endured an assault to his brain via a hammer because this MAGA budmash demanded to kill his wife, Nancy Pelosi. Hope is not moot within the Americas because Luiz Inácio Lula da Silva defeated the far-right wing incumbent, President Jair Bolsonaro of Brazil. Furthermore, a failed coup that replicates America's January 6, 2021 fiasco was rendered futile. Hence, Brazil dodged the bullet of fascism this time.

As a caveat, to the right wing party in Israel, please cease and desist with your war on Palestine! Don't create an

Arab Holocaust on the Palestinian people because you know first-hand what the deadly ramifications and effects of attempted genocide are and the havoc it reaps long after this assault happens. There is no rationalization for any global holocaust anywhere on this planet regardless of who initiated the conflict. I am an author that espouses world peace and the Middle East is no exception, so no more war. No group of humans are 'chosen' over any other group of individuals because we are equal to all organisms within the eyes of our universe.

There is nothing new under the sun because the winds of change are always among us. As a spiritual being incarnated as a female African human, I will subconsciously apply and savor my experiences to evoke compassion and love towards others when I encounter my next incarnation. When we deeply examine our Deoxyribonucleic Acid (DNA) and compare its design with our primordial cosmos (galaxies, star systems, nebulae, black holes and etcetera), we will realize that each of us are little universes. Thus, there is never a need to get too attached to anything when we know it will always metamorphose into something else because this is an aspect of universal law. Beauteous butterflies exemplify this miraculous process. Amazingly, the DNA inside a caterpillar before it alchemizes into a butterfly is completely different. Resisting flux is a fruitless notion that brings nothing into fruition, but chaos and stagnation. Furthermore, change is our only constant and another universal law. So, let's just go with the flow and transcend our egos because we are eternal luminosities.

'Cherry Blossom Blues' ♪♫ is Historical Fiction dedicated to my true loves: Jasper and Jett.

Chapter 1
"I Shall Be Released"
by Nina Simone

The majestic and mighty Queen Elizabeth II of the United Kingdom tersely summarized my Earthly existence to a tee by coining this phrase: *Grief is the price we pay for love.* Reflecting back on my life is like watching a picture show divulging fast-moving flashbacks, now that death is nigh. One of the harshest winters that I can remember is in 1899. Street cars stall along O Street, where we live. Water pipes burst; icicles ornately adorn houses as long, glistening and sharp Samurai swords dangling high from the rooftops. Streets appeared as brackish ice…dangerous and dirty causing fatal car crashes, horse drawn carriage accidents and falls. The U.S. Capitol is buried under the bombardment of incessant snow. The Bushbury electric cars are stalled or stopped in time. New Year's Eve is slowly approaching. Everyone will be glad to bring in the new year: 1900, which is a brand-new century: the 20th. This specific time is particularly special. I was born during the Gilded Age, or shall we call it the Gaudy Era? Opulence and extravagance are the name of the game. Perhaps these outer beautifications and formalities are facades to clandestinely hide the evil that lurks within so many edifices and people during this epoque. The wealthy class is augmented by leaps of innovative technology. It is an exciting time to be alive. The advent of new communication inventions: the phonograph, the telephone, radio, newspapers, magazines and film coupled with recently developed sports: basketball, bicycling, and football. Also, advanced transportation machinery is introduced, such as automobiles, electric trains and trolleys. I liken these unconventional conveniences to living in the future due to their dreamlike qualities.

My mother always adorns herself with the Beltless wrapper dresses, while my sister would sport the Gibson girl look. My parents are both graduates of Howard University. Our family milieu is affluent yet, superficial. The custom is that Negroes who could attend this prestigious institution had to pass the paper bag test. Or, one's complexion must be lighter than a paper bag to matriculate into Howard University. Yes, this is a pedagogical place for passing Negroes, high-yellow niggas, redbones, mulattoes, children of mulattoes and octoroons. Never mind, measuring the person's intelligence or integrity because the only criterion for matriculation is based on the magnitude of lightness one's physical complexion could attain. Obtaining a 'Mrs. degree' by many high yellow women is the primary reason they even go to college because their sole desire is to marry a wealthy husband. Predictably, most of these entrappers never attain a university degree for themselves. Hence, the curse of the color barrier permits redbones to always reach the top tiers of society. The analogy of house Negros versus field Negros is the same stark contrast upheld within most social stratifications within the Afro-American community. For the most part, fair skinned Black women marry well-to-do Afro-American men. This is simply the expectation. In rare cases, where they would be able to marry White men is to live the ultimate entitled life. Prayerfully, their offspring will not reveal their latent African DNA. Regrettably, this shameful aspect is an indelible imprint of Negro culture. My father was born and raised in Gouldtown, New Jersey. He has blue, slightly bulging eyes and he is crowned with thin, straight, dirty blond hair. His lips are almost non-existent, while he sports permanent rose cheeks, highlighting his chiseled nose with a creamy vanilla skinned backdrop peppered with faint brown freckles sloping atop his profoundly high cheek bones. Like father, like son, because the majority of women constantly chased after him. My mother was not one of those participants because he persistently pursued her instead. Gouldtown, is located outside of Philadelphia; it is the first and oldest mulatto municipality where most of their population intermarry relatives to keep their families light and bright. Above all, it is taboo for them to marry anyone who is deemed dark-skinned. This ideology also applied to my family and many other fair-skinned Blacks by ensuring that our offspring will always be light enough to perpetuate the privileges bestowed upon us by Whites. We are never equal to Caucasians, but we accept the crumbs given to us by Whites to be superior to darker-skinned Blacks. This vicious cycle continues without consciously realizing that we are promoting White supremacy by ingesting the same false narrative that the lack of melanization, a natural occurring molecule in nature, is a beauty standard. Rumors spread that preserving colorism is so widespread that first cousins would marry and procreate together to simply ensure having light skinned children in Gouldtown. Imagine, involving incest to maintain appearances. How sick and perverse is this! Maintaining brightness in the family must be a powerful priority. We also heard hearsay that my father's lineage owned Negro slaves about two generations ago. Yes, Coloreds owning Negroes, like themselves, but we did not have any concrete proof. In any event, my father could frequent as many 'White Only' stores in Maryland and Virginia without evoking any suspicion from anyone whilst always buying us the finest merchandise. My father is a civil engineer, while my mother has a degree in Home Economics, she prefers to be a stay-at-home wife and mother. My family is very bourgeois and we always had the finest comforts. My mother prefers to use the verbiage literati instead of bourgeoisie. Unlike my father, she is a native of Washington, D.C. My mother adorns an hourglass and a very voluptuous figure. The nation's capital is infamous for having a plethora of high-yellow Blacks residing in its midst. Most people could only afford horse-drawn carriages, but we proudly owned a green 1899 Sperry Electric Runabout. Electricity is finally tamed and the new miracle on the planet. Light beyond candles and gas lamps are inside businesses and residences. Thomas Alva Edison keeps inventing exciting devices. However, Lewis H. Latimer, a Negro is responsible for the advent of the lightbulb. Edison's overshadowing of Latimer's genius is no surprise living in the United States of America. In any event, it is awe-inspiring to have harnessed electricity from thunder storms and put it inside of our homes, regardless of who gets the credit for it! We live in Georgetown, where our family would always gather around the huge phonograph in our Florida Room. We would play Scott Joplin's 'The Entertainer' over and over…I recall counting 20 uninterrupted intervals. These were great times. Slavery ended about 30 years past. My family was not considered 'Black' because we were so fair-skinned. I am sure that we descended from a slave somewhere back in time, but this part of Afro-American history was very remote for us to comprehend. My father passes as a White man; alternatively, my mother is high-yellow, or very light-skinned; she could never pass for a Caucasian woman because her facial features are profoundly Negroid. She has viscous lips and a wide, flat nose. My sister and I could not pass for the White race either. My sister, Holly's hair is too kinky; you could barely get a comb through it. It is long and thick. She had to get her hair straightened with a hot iron comb just to manage it. I had my mother's nose. People who know me call me 'Peanut'. My birth name is Hunter Axel Williams. According to my parents, their lineage and heritage has always been free. Furthermore, they don't recall having enslaved ancestry. We live in a section of Georgetown where most of the occupants are passing to light-skinned Black families mixed along with some Jewish White upper middle-class ones. During this time, most of the United States is comprised of an elite group of Blacks having fair skin who dwell in the upper echelon castes of society in comparison to darker skinned Afro-Americans. Later, I learn that colorism within the African diaspora is a comprehensive caste system. One could see the Potomac River as our backyard. We are Lutheran, but we only go to church during the Christmas holidays and Easter. However, we have one neighbor whose family has a dark complexion. They are Freedmen who migrated from Macon, Georgia. Their father owns his own cobbler store. Their business could cobble all kinds of shoes from the Balmoral boot to the ball-bearing bicycle shoe and everything in between. Most impressively, they restore everything extremely well. Their surname is Widgeon. Their family comprises the mother, father, and three children. I am 10 years old and I would turn 11 on January 2nd. There are two girls and a boy. I never really could focus on what the sisters look like, but I guess one would say that they are attractive. The brother is one of the most beautiful creatures that I ever laid eyes on. His skin is so rich and pure, like dark chocolate. He has Semitic features; he resembles an Ethiopian or a person from southern India. He is maybe 11 or older. I am not sure, but I could see him every evening in his bedroom due to his candlelit lamp. I always anxiously anticipated the night because it gave sight to such a gorgeous young man. After weeks of watching and observing this inky, statuesque figure, we finally introduce ourselves. The blizzard subsided, while the sun shines brightly and brilliantly throughout the day. He sat on his porch holding a drink, of something, so I decided to go over to his house and introduce myself.

"Welcome to the neighborhood! I am Hunter, but my friends call me 'Peanut'. What's your name?"

"I am Barrington."

"How old are you?"

"I am 11. What's your age?"

"I am 10, but I'll be 11 next month."

Barrington is rather reserved. He would rarely initiate eye contact. His answers to my inquiries are brief and guarded. He sipped hot chocolate with marshmallows; he said that this is his favorite beverage. We always make eye contact with one another. Our parents are cordial, but they never invite each other to their respective residences. 'Hi and Bye' is the entirety of their meetings and greetings. My kin never spews a negative word regarding Barrington's family, yet they never encourage our friendship either.

Christmas day is here. My mother always ensures that we have color-coordinated napery for every holiday. We have a maid who is very dark-skinned; her name is Alma. She prepares the best meals. My mother and father always insist on Western European cuisine. My mother takes charge of the table setting. We dine on the finest China, but our silverware and dinnerware originate from Japan. The silverware is made from 24 karat gold and our plates are comprised of porcelain. I deem the most beautiful items on the table are the crystal glass flutes. My mother and father love to boast about how this fine tableware arrived on the Abyssinia. Every holiday, the menu stays the same. Sweetbreads, or cow throats are the appetizer. Beef wellington is the main dish, accompanied with roasted Brussel sprouts, macaroni and cheese and grounded cranberries. The elixirs for the adults are Jack Rose, but the underage drink milk or Sarsaparilla. Holly and I have to always sit at the children's table, or kiddy table because we are not allowed to sit at the grand buffet with the adults. If the weather permits, we will have Christmas carolers sing to us within our community. I really believe that our four-legged beloved cats, Max and Mimi, have the most fun. I love watching them attempt to climb our 10-foot Balsam Fir gallantly standing in our living room.

We always had to have a real Christmas tree because my mother just loves the smell of natural pine. My father adorned my mother with a new mink coat, while my sister was given a pair of roller skates, while I received a bicycle. We bought our father new leather boots for work. Unlike our family, Barrington's folks do not celebrate Christmas. They had no decorations, a Christmas tree, or the custom of exchanging gifts. There is a quiet dignity emanating around Barrington's family. They have no formal education, but they amass many material things of quality. Strangely, Sunday evenings around 7 p.m., I could see multiple candles burning from the windows in the basement from Barrington's home. Barrington's residence would have around 10 to 12 visitors arrive. We live in three-story rowhouses. My parents would whisper about the strange lights seen through our neighbor's windows, but they were quite indifferent about the entire exhibit. One night, I saw floating orbs of bright lights —they are distinct from the many candles burning. My befuddlement was transfixed by my fatigue. Then, I noticed that these balls of luminosity happen every time Barrington's family have these Sunday gatherings.

The holidays flew by, as usual. Barrington and I became associates. I invited him to my birthday celebration. We had my favorite cake: chocolate fudge with marshmallow cream. Months passed, and Barrington and I would mostly assemble during the weekends because we attend different schools. I go to Friends school, which is private, while Barrington frequents a public school. I finally felt comfortable to ask him about the candle Sunday sessions at his house. He smirked and uttered, "They are séances."

"What's that?" I blurted in ignorance.

"It's a way of communicating with our dearly departed."

"You mean…Dead people!"

"Yes," Barrington commented. I was raised to know that death is an illusion. People simply transition to another dimension. Death is nothing more than a doorway, or portal to another place and time. The soul dwells completely in the astral plane, totally void of our egos. Séances reveal the multiverse, where science only hypothesizes about it. I had a twin brother, Byron, who died. We were playing basketball on a huge ice pond about 30 yonder from here on a very bone-chilling afternoon. The ball cracked a compromised section of the ice pond when my brother fell into the freezing water. I tried to save him, but I couldn't because I slipped. Amazingly, this pond had seiches, similar to undertows. When I fell, Byron floated under the remaining ice sheet. I tried to break it, but it was too dense. I used a rock and a rotted tree trunk, but nothing would open the hardened ice. The tips of my fingers began to burn after experiencing a numbing sensation because I wore no gloves. I feared that I had frost bite. So, I ran home, as fast as I could to get help. By the time, my Pa arrived, Byron drowned. I didn't speak for an entire year.

Paradoxical to their beliefs, my family thought Heaven and Hell are the only two places to greet humanity upon death. His talk regarding egos went above my head. *Poor,*

Barrington, I thought to myself. My sister is my best friend. I don't know what I would do if I lost her. He made it very clear to me to not pity him because he is in close contact with Byron. The séances reveal how Byron is faring on the other side. Byron is doing quite well. Barrington always stresses that our 'dearly departed' are always watching and protecting their living relatives, so never be sad because they are always with us.

"What religion is your family?" I asked.

Barrington sternly scoffs, "My family avows no religion. Alternatively, we are spiritualists. We are of the opinion that all living things possess a soul. Thus, we are spiritual beings experiencing the life form of a human incarnation. Or, we can be spiritual beings living as a cat, worm, rock and etcetera."

Years later, I researched the epistemology of the Widgeon family, which is based on the tenets of Emanuel Swedenborg. I always enjoy eating at Barrington's home because they eat soul food: ham hocks, shrimp and grits, collard greens, black-eye peas, sweet potatoes, chitterlings, potato salad and fried chicken. My family never eats this genre of eatables. I thought our food is so bland and each dining interaction is too formal. Every breakfast consists of cream of wheat with milk, or soft-boiled eggs with buttered toast.

A decade later, Barrington and I still remain close friends. I would often gratify myself whenever I visualize Barrington before I go to bed. I'd usually have to cover my mouth in order to prevent my screams from alarming my family members during my nightly orgasms. Barrington asked me a rather odd inquiry while riding the streetcar together in Washington, DC during the late afternoon.

"Byron said that you are in love with me. Is this true?"

I was absolutely speechless. I didn't know what to say.

"Tell me the truth, Peanut. He recounted this to me around 10 years ago."

"It is true. I was afraid to let you know because I was not sure if you were gay, or even felt the same about me," I whispered.

"You fooled me because you had so many girls chasing you all of the time. It seemed like you enjoyed the attention from them," Barrington insisted.

I listened intently to Barrington's every word as I smile like Mona Lisa's portrait. My heart exults with pure delight. Little did Barrington know; I had no interest in any of those frivolous females trying to court me. However, I relish the covert protection of my sexual status due to all of the womanly enthrallment that I receive. Barrington confesses that he is gay too. There is nothing effeminate about Barrington or myself. Thus, our outward appearances are about as masculine as any man can be. We could never openly express our sexual orientations because the paradigm, or narrative, is that homosexuality is comparable to mental illness. I deem this prognosis to be a ludicrous notion because I am one of the most logical people that I know on Earth. Another stereotype that I wholeheartedly disavow is that women are subservient to men. My mother and sister are two of the strongest people that exist. Furthermore, I wonder how many people would populate the planet if men solely had to give birth, as I laugh to myself. I don't agree with any of these widespread tropes.

We never acted on our sexual orientations. Since these confessions to one another, we always cuddled in either his bed or mine being fully clothed at each other's houses when possible. We conversed intimately with one another for hours. I loved both of my cats, but I have a proclivity towards Max. I delight falling asleep to his peaceful and piercing purring. I would often hold him and think about Barrington.

My parents want me to get engaged to a woman that I took to the annual cotillion. Heather is rather striking. She is tall, thin, argent-colored and has soft, long, light-brown hair. Her eyes are hazel and she definitely passes for White. There is so much pressure from both of our families to get married. The following year, we tied the knot. Our wedding was small and intimate. I invited Barrington to come and he did.

After the reception ended, Barrington and I went for a long walk together along the Potomac River. We held one another and tongue kissed, while we grinded roughly against our penises facing each other. Barrington has a very thick cock with a huge circumference and girth. While mine is long, like a cobra. Our breathing is so labored and lusty. In the heat of the moment, I had anal sex with Barrington behind some bushes. I had to wet my hands with my own saliva before putting my penis into Barrington's anus to ensure that our sexual experience was as pleasurable as possible. My penis is so hard and erect that one could see the actual veins swell, like raging river rapids. My entire body gyrates from the entire experience; it will not stop shaking to the subtlest touch. Barrington performed oral sex on me, slowly kissing my penis and then put my entire male genitalia inside of his mouth sucking it in an upward and downward fashion. Tears streamed down our visages due to the amplified intensity. The sensations rise subtly to soothing, then they hasten to a crescendo of optimal euphoria. During climax, my toes start to curl. This transgression is like having a religious epiphany. This is our first sexual experience. The thought of returning to Heather that evening makes me dismally depressed. On a positive note, I can close my eyes and pretend that she is Barrington when I have to have sex with her.

On January 6, 1910 the first Cherry Blossom trees arrive from Japan as a gift to our government on the Potomac River. Only four days after my birthday, what a glorious celebration. Unfortunately, they have an insect infestation and are destroyed by fire. To my consternation, this horrific incident will symbolize my life for years to come. I follow the tradition of my parents and attended Howard University. I was not sure of what I want to study, but religion fascinates me. There is a myriad of doctrines around the world, so I thought that I should immerse myself into this field of study. My parents sharply disapprove because they contend that no significant amount of money could be garnished with this particular major. I didn't care and I wasn't looking for their validation either. If they did not want to pay for my collegiate education, then I would pursue other endeavors.

Barrington went to trade school to become proficient in plumbing and have an electrician certification. I thought to myself that this is a very practical and useful ambition. Barrington married a girl that he was dating for some time the following year. She is quite attractive, brown-skinned and tall. Her name is Meredith. Their wedding was simple yet very elegant. Many of the people that attended this auspicious event, are the same people who frequented his family's numerous séances.

The Widgeon's gleaned the art of having séances from their former slave owners who were strict followers of mesmerism. This ideology crested because so many Southerners had no idea of the happenings to their family and friends during the Civil War. Their slaveowners were actually very just compared to most enslavers in Macon, Georgia. The Widgeon's (slaveholders) rarely even physically beat their slaves or abused them in any fashion. Their paradoxical practices allowed Barrington's family to purchase their freedom before the Emancipation Proclamation. Once Barrington's paternal grandfather was granted his freedom, he took his entire family and moved to Washington, DC. In March of 1912, the mayor of Tokyo, Yukio Ozaki, gave 3,000 new cherry blossom trees to our nation's capital. Miraculously, these arboreal beings are free of any parasites. Interestingly, 1912 is a leap year, with the consumption of alcoholic beverages on the rise. Women drinking in public is normalized. My wife had her share of inebriated socially exposed encounters. Heather is never quiet or pleasantly pot-valiant; instead, she is boisterous and brutal. When she is sober, she is so classy and kind. After her fill of gin, she would aggressively hurl profane language at me or anyone who happens to be in her company.

"You fuckin' muthafucka, why don't you get a real fuckin' job instead of mimicking a gotdamn preacher! You ain't shit, you bullshittin', useless muthafucka!" Heather spewed in slurred speech and a staggered swagger.

As far as I am concerned, our marriage was a sham from the start. When I met Heather, she didn't drink, at least to my knowledge. The following mornings, she never remembers the horrible things that she does or says. I had to know, so I inquired. "When did you start boozing?"

"Playing pinochle with my girlfriends every Saturday evening," Heather declares.

"You've only been drinking for about two years now."

"Yes, that's about right," she agreed. "We drank absinthe mixed with champagne, but our lovely government just banned absinthe, so our club meetings replaced it with gin this year."

I suggested that she shouldn't consume alcohol because it makes her too belligerent. Heather agreed with me because whenever I confronted her regarding her dastardly deeds, she can never recall anything. Furthermore, Heather only made empty promises because she continues to drink wherever and whenever she can. Her charming and kind verbiage would transmute into pure vitriol. Her drinking became so intolerable that my family suggested that she be institutionalized in an asylum. Barrington is so lucky because his wife did not engage in such pursuits. Meredith is a wonderful homemaker, wife and mother. Unlike Heather and I, Barrington and Meredith have a son: Marcus. Heather and I barely have sex and now her obsession with liquor consumption is obstructing her fertility. Heather was never domesticated because her family has a maid to do their house chores. She is only expected to look pretty and marry a man of means. Most beautiful women are deluded to think that their beauty is eternal when their physical looks have an expiration date. They have become so acclimated to people being enthralled and kowtowing to them because of their good looks that they forget they are only temporal. Often, they neglect to enhance and nurture their inner beauty.

I found metal flasks inside of Heather's purses, under our towels in the bathroom and even inside her shoes in our bedroom closet. All of the them filled with gin. I became accustomed to Heather's drunkenness inside of our home, but she started disappearing for days. I feel so helpless. I did not know where to look for her, so I just waited for Heather to come home. When she did return to our residence, she was disheveled and tried to conceal her staggering saunter. Perhaps my lack of ingesting alcoholic beverages made Heather feel uncomfortable. My decision not to partake in recreational drinking is simply because I detest the taste of any liquors…it is not a moral judgement. Like myself, Meredith and Barrington do not abuse alcohol. We are very responsible social drinkers. Meredith was a singer for the Fisk Jubilee Choir. She met Barrington while on tour, visiting the nation's capital. Barrington recalls that Meredith's voice simulated angels in heaven. After watching a Christmas performance with her singing a solo, 'Deep River', on stage accompanied by a harp in concert, he knew that she would be the perfect wife for him. Meredith travelled to Europe and sang for royalty in England and the Netherlands. She is quite cultured. Meredith even performed in Joplin's iconic opera entitled, Treemonisha. Meredith is so gracious because she gave me a phonograph of Treemonisha. I never heard anything about it; I own a lot of Joplin's musical work. In any event, I fell in love with it on my first listen. Ironically, I put Heather in an asylum with hopes of curing her booze intake. I did not make this decision alone because I consulted with her family, and we agreed that it was the best thing to do to ensure her safety. When it rains, it pours. My mother apprised me that Mimi died in her sleep. She was 21 years old. I buried her in my parent's backyard. Three months later, Max transitioned. He lived to the ripe age of 22. Their graves are next to one another, labelled by a makeshift headstone made of sandstone with their names as their insignia. The melancholy I have is overwhelming. I vividly remember finding both of my cats in an alley way not far from my childhood abode. I consult Barrington about doing a séance to be with my cats again. He utters that they never communed with dead animals, but he would make a special attempt for me. He told me to bring personal objects of the cats, like their toys or something that absorbed their energy or essence. I confided to Holly about having a séance for our cats. She roared with laughter, as loud as a lion, and agreed. Fortnight to the day, I confirmed the séance to my sister. The four of us conducted it in the home of Barrington's parents. It consisted of the four of us: myself, Meredith, Holly and Barrington. I brought my cats' milk bowl and a toy mouse that they would attack and chew. The moment has finally arrived; this is my first séance. The four of us hold hands and call their names: Mimi and Max. The lit candles flutter wildly, and Barrington's chandelier swings violently from side to side. I did not see anything, but I hear their meows. The hairs on the nape of my neck abruptly rise. Max is the loudest; Mimi meows shortly after Max. Barrington said that they departed and the entire séance is consummated.

"Did you see them?" I hastily implore.

"No," everyone replies in unison, but "we sure did hear them!" Without hesitation, we burst into a thunderous laughter.

Whenever an entity arrives during a séance, the temperature in the room significantly plummets to almost a freezing point. This is no exaggeration! In addition, strange and muted smells waft through the surrounding air, as if daring to introduce themselves. Because our eyes are always shut, our remaining senses become more pronounced and keener. The Widgeons have another nemesis besides Hoover in which to hide under the radar. The famous magician: Harry Houdini's obsessive and relentless pursuits of authenticating fraudulent séances via Spiritualism is attempting to enact laws in Congress against spiritual shams. This is becoming a political witch hunt, much like the beautiful, liberated and strong women endured during the Salem trials in 1692! As an outsider, I know that Barrington's séances are really real. Furthermore, I am a skeptic regarding any spiritual principles. Luckily, Barrington's séances remain out-of-sight during Houdini's staunch and irrational attempts to eradicate this much needed spiritual practice that unites the living with our departed loved ones. To make matters worse, the press continues to cover and highlight Houdini's hostility towards séances. Houdini, the ghost buster, lacks any objective discernment between genuine séances versus disingenuous ones. His vicious attacks are directed toward all séances. By waging his caustic war in support of banning this spiritual practice, people in all dimensions will suffer. Houdini's rageful rants only dissipated from the ether because no followers of Spiritualism were ever legally persecuted or punished for practicing our religious beliefs. However, some family reputations are unethically vitiated.

Barrington and I still live in Georgetown, but we purchased our own rowhouses. We also bought the 1910 Ford Model T cars. Barrington's is red and I have a green one. I am so fortunate to have a great friend, like Barrington. He is loyal; could keep secrets and he has the skillset to fix cars. Meredith's parents called her to inform her about her father's health in Nashville, Tennessee. Her father fell ill with consumption, so Meredith decided to take Marcus and stay with her parents for a few weeks. She took the train to be with her dad during his dying days. In Meredith's absence, Barrington and I had entire nights, days, and mornings to spend together. My love for him spans over a decade. We cuddled, bathed and made love to one another. It is as if we are married. I wish that would be the case, but of course this notion is impossible. I adored living with Barrington. We cooked, cleaned, played chess and listened to the radio and phonograph together. Every morning, we awoke together by straddling each other's body and offered a peck on our foreheads. I surmised that we are so natural together. Those two and a half weeks flew by; Meredith and Marcus are back at home. Sadly, her father died and they had a small funeral for him. There was not enough time for Barrington to take the train and make the funeral on time, so he sent floral arrangements and cards instead. He revealed to me that he cared deeply for Meredith. I told him that it is quite conspicuous and they are blessed to have one another. I confess to him that I am totally indifferent towards Heather. I tried to show overt care, but it is feigned.

Instead of calling, I went by the asylum to visit Heather. It has been a month, and Heather looks radiant. She alerted me that the psychiatrist does not think that she is ready to leave the facility.

"Why?" I replied.

She exclaimed that she still desires drinking cocktails.

"This place can't make me stop. You, No one can," she smirked facetiously. "Only me and I don't want to quit drinking. I enjoy it too much," Heather confessed.

"You must be planning on living here then for your remaining days, with this attitude," I leered.

"Not hardly. When I am ready to leave, I will finagle the staff of just that," she ogled.

"Heather, you must take some sort of culpability, as to why you are here," I laughingly scoffed.

I don't have the wherewithal to keep Heather indefinitely inside this asylum. We exchanged our goodbyes without a single physical touch between us. Heather's feckless and entitled personality is so off-putting! I simply can't stand her! On a brighter note, I went to visit Holly and my parents. They briefly asked about Heather's condition. I let them know that she refuses to get better. This is her choice and she will have to live with it.

I relish my freedom by having the house to myself. I preferred to be alone than be with Heather. Life is good. When Heather was eventually released from the asylum, she went to live with her parents. We never legally divorced, but we should have. She continues to drink profusely and her folks enable her, as usual. We went our separate ways and lived our own lives apart from one another. I was rewarded a job as a philosophy professor at Howard

University with tenure. Barrington continues to maintain and sustain his father's family business. Yet, he expanded it from shoe repairs and added automobiles to his repertoire. His business is burgeoning too. Barrington and his wife follow a leader known as Marcus Garvey in Harlem, New York. Harlem is the rage at this time and the place of Black excellence, in terms of education, culture and polity. Barrington is planning on relocating his family outside of the United States due to White terrorism still occurring inside this country. Most newspapers would report hangings of Black men, children and women by the hands of Ku Klux Klan members throughout the South. Moreover, the insidious Eugenics movement also flourishes in the 1920s. Decades later, Nazis would emulate and adopt the United States' use of Eugenics to murder over six million innocent Jews in Europe. On April 12, 1924, the United States passes the Johnson-Reed Act, which restricts primarily Japanese, Jewish descendants, and eastern and southern Europeans from immigrating into America. Thus, the quota emigration system from certain countries is deemed as keeping our nation racially pure, as opposed to being overrun by Mongols. Even during the later years of the 1920s, Congress passes the Undesirable Aliens Act of 1929 (Blease' Law) Section 1325 of Title 8, which criminalizes Mexicans for attempting border crossings. Xenophobia is a lasting scaffold that continues to scar and mar our great nation. Why is no surprise because people in power want to preserve the White Anglo-Saxon Protestant (WASP) gene pool within the United States. In retrospect, this is definitely a decade of cataclysmic contrasts!

"The white devil does not care how light and bright you are. You will never be fully invited to white people's club because they perceive you only as a hybrid of their whiteness. The glass ceiling is always present for you. Remember, the One Drop Rule in this evil country we call The United States of America is rooted in hatred just not of the African diaspora, but all people of color, including Semites," Barrington vented. "Furthermore, they intend to use your kind as peons to enforce whatever schemes they unfold to maintain and sustain their global power throughout the world."

"Garvey's teachings espouse that Africans of the diaspora can only attain dignity, freedom, and safety by living solely outside of the United States of America. Because no matter how many laws are passed to protect Negros and Native Americans, the majority of the hearts and minds of the 'powers that be' are deeply rooted to destroy the progress of Afro-Americans and other people of color in the USA. This will never change. Garvey is a huge proponent of separatism of the races, and this is the overwhelming commonality that he shares with the KKK," Barrington exclaimed.

Barrington's family became Pan-Africanists; they are determined to emigrate outside of the United States. I refuse to join the United Negro Improvement Association (UNIA) because my family and myself are flourishing. Barrington's company is thriving too, so I am perplexed as to why Barrington shows such commitment and compassion for the Marcus Garvey movement. Alternatively, I am not condoning hangings or racism towards the African diaspora; I just want Black people to fight for what is rightfully ours in the United States. This is the only home that I know, and I do not feel comfortable living in a foreign country outside of the USA. Barrington's family is rarely in Washington, DC because they are always travelling to New York City to aid Garvey's organization. The beautiful and regal family of three traverse the train from Manhattan to Washington, DC, and vice versa. I could not resist, so I introduced this topic to my students at Howard University. For my classes' finals, they have to write a dissertation regarding should Black Americans be totally independent of White society, premised upon Marcus Garvey? Why or why not? Is this a realistic notion to be accomplished? What are the benefits and pitfalls that you foresee within this radical societal norm?

Barrington requested that I keep an eye on his property since his family is frequently traveling to New York City for the Marcus Garvey conferences. I notice something very strange and foreboding: White men dressed in black suits entering and exiting his residence. I could tell that they were not the local police force. They took pictures with vest pocket kodak cameras throughout Barrington's house. This whole scenario is insidious. I gaze from afar to make sure that I was out of sight, but I still could observe what was happening. I alerted Barrington by calling him at his hotel about this predicament when I returned to my lodging. When we converse, Barrington said that Garvey warned us that the Federal Bureau of Investigation would investigate and harass his devotees. J. Edgar Hoover is obsessed with the causes of Marcus Garvey because Garvey wants to dismantle white supremacy and empower Black people all over the world. Barrington's family is already prepared for

Hoover's irrational raids. Thus, they never keep any confidential information at their residence when they are gone. Hoover is as persistent with his FBI raids, as a New York City tenement cockroach is on the hunt for food. Unlike the Jewish, Irish and Italian mobs, Garvey's movement is just, noble and legal. Barrington and I agree that Hoover should focus his attention on these crime organizations flooding our nation with illegal liquor and unnecessary deadly violence, as opposed to stalking Marcus Garvey without any legitimate causes. Every day, the newspapers report people being assassinated via gun violence in the streets in front of women and children in broad daylight. The killings by these mobsters are absolutely senseless! Blood and gore welcome everyone, wherever you go. Hence, no one is safe!

"These mobsters are all white. The law has a higher standard for these types of criminals. Arrests aren't a priority for them," Barrington proclaims.

Pensively, I concurred that Black lives don't matter here in the United States and that Barrington is so right regarding the intricacies and nuances of racism. We live in the heart of our nation's government: Washington DC, where President Woodrow Wilson openly hates the Afro-American. Wilson purported an untrue film of fiction depicting Coloreds with degradation and had the gall to attempt to effectuate it into a factual documentary. In February of 1915, he had a special White House screening of 'The Birth of a Nation', where he had the audacity to remark, "It's like writing history with lightning. My only regret is that it is all so terribly true."

How sick and unpresidential is this?! The president of the United States of America is an open bigot who makes no bones about hating Negros publicly. My peers at Howard University devised plans on how to instruct this insidiousness to our students. We entitled it, "White Supremacy thrives in the highest office in the land." By mingling with whites, black people are denied too many opportunities. My hometown is known as 'chocolate city' due to the influx of Blacks living in Washington, DC, yet we don't have a Black president serving us here. My cultural sphere has been so limited because I live, work, and play around my own community. I know whites exist, but my family and many other 'Black families' that I am familiar with congregate with our own, not outside of our race. We are very content with this fact. I don't want to be a hypocrite because my fair skin affords me opportunities to accomplish more in American society than my darker skinned counterparts. I never really feel comfortable discussing the problem of 'colorism' with Barrington, yet he openly converses with me on the subject matter. Barrington would always emphasize that White supremacy utilizes the strategy of divide and conquer by pitting subgroups against one another and creating self-hatred of our ethnicity by promoting a love and admiration of their white race. I am a member of the National Association for the Advancement of Colored People (NAACP) created by W.E.B. Du Bois and Ida B Wells. This organization is enough to satisfy and quell my needs for making a difference via racial oppression. Harlem is the epicenter of Black culture and Afro-intelligentsia. Headquartered here are literature, music, and social organizations for change.

The prevalence of misogyny continues to climb our societal vine. August 28, 1917, is a day to live forever in infamy because Wilson enforces the arrests of hundreds of women in the suffrage movement who innocently protest their civil rights to vote outside of the White House. Some victims spent days, weeks and months in prisons where they are served rotten food laced with worms and other vermin. The degree of police savagery towards these females is outrageous because women are tugged away, kicking and screaming as officers tear their dresses, pull their hair, punch their bodies and literally throw them inside of the plethora of paddy wagons awaiting them. These egregious acts are done in broad daylight without any reprisal. I want to intervene, but as a black man, the cops might shoot and kill me. These weak men don't care who sees them committing these unparallel acts of flagrant police brutality. Despite the farce and travesty of these trumped charges, these brave muliebral beings continue to march outside of the White House, promoting female voting on a daily basis sharing an unstoppable movement to mobilize change via the American political system. These ungodly efforts to obstruct women's rights is to no avail because on August 18, 1920, women finally have equal rights in regards to voting with men. Derisively, the 19th amendment is designed exclusively for women of European descent, not melanated ones. Racism relentlessly rears its ugly head because Anglo-American women covet their right to vote without making any sacrifices or concessions for their melanated sisters: Asian, Latino, Afro-American, and Native American to also have their political freedoms. This is why Ida B. Wells-Barnett takes the helm and reigns over this affray for voting rights for all women. Some of the hypocrisy that White women exhibit towards Colored women is ferociously infuriating. Barnett is a great friend of Barrington, so them to his future lineages, is an honor to hear and see her first-hand accounts of this specific microcosmic struggle when I visit him in Harlem.

I find myself staring at our wedding photographs. Heather and I do make a stunningly handsome couple. Her wedding dress, my tuxedo, the floral bouquets, and the design of the cake are perfect. I admonish myself for even getting married in the first place; our marriage is a farce from the start. I wish that same-sex marriages are legal, but I can only dream for that day to manifest itself because I only want to be with Barrington. I pondered his reciprocation of our relationship. I don't know if it's an act, but Barrington appears natural and content with Meredith and his son Marcus. Ostensibly, they have the perfect family. The White Widgeon slave owners taught Barrington's grandfather, Otis, everything regarding the spiritual realm from familiars, omens, spells, and even tarot cards. Barrington's grandfather grew so adept with his supernatural skills that he earned a living entertaining other slaves with his newly learned Black magic. Slave master Widgeon was so impressed that Otis would uphold his traditions with such dignity and esteem that he granted him and his entire family their freedom through the Homestead Act. As long as Otis would keep his séance traditions sacred and teach them to his future lineages, he didn't even have to buy his freedom. Auspiciously, Mr. Widgeon gave it to them for their occult patronage. He even offered Otis and his family one acre of land, housing and some farm animals.

Technically, Otis was a sharecropper who did not have to pay rent for his land and his other ownerships. Otis deeply appreciated this wonderful opportunity, but he eventually wanted to spread his wings and leave Macon, Georgia to head North because there was no amount of metaphysical protection in the world to stop the numerous lynchings transpiring to black men, women and children in the South. Otis was only three years old when he watched his father die by being hung from a cherry blossom tree. Years later, in 1949, Macon will become the cherry blossom tree capital of the world giving Washington, DC a run for its money. Otis' dad is named Rufus. Rufus, or Barrington's grandfather was only trying to escape by taking his freedom, as opposed to bargaining for it. The little bit of food that he stole would only last a few days. Rufus was missing for two weeks. He slept inside some of the Ocmulgee mounds, but he chose to trail the Ocmulgee river in order to conceal his scent from the bloodhounds. Slave patrols (modern day policemen) on horseback and dogs tracked Rufus down by the riverbank. The soles of his feet were slashed from thorned plants; he survived a poisonous cottonmouth snake bite and endured the freezing nights. In spite of all of his efforts, he could not outrun the salacious slave catchers. Rufus always used the same phrase to appeal to his slave masters.

"Massa, I's a good boy, pleez don't whoop ma, Massa," Rufus incessantly pleaded. However, his numerous pleas fell on deaf ears because they tarred and feathered Rufus when they brought him back to the plantation. To make matters worse, he was tortured by burning his raw cuts on the soles of his feet with fire torches. His legs and feet were skinned, then his ears were removed with a knife before they put a rope around his neck. Otis vividly remembers that his father's half-burned and tarred body was such an unnatural, lifeless appendage attaching itself to a beautiful, breathing, blossoming cherry tree. All the while, white families with children cheered and took photographs of this gruesome event. Despairingly, this contradictory visual became an indelible one for Otis, not to mention the smelly putridity of burnt, decomposing human flesh.

Chapter 2
"Love's in Need of Love Today" by Stevie Wonder

The United States is not the only country consumed with violence; the entire world is now plagued with it. There is great instability in the air…nations pitted against nations. With the current confluences, it is a very unsettling time; it seems like the end of the world according to 'Revelations' in the Bible. Great Britain and The United States declare war on Prussia, coupled with the Russian revolution with the Communist Bolsheviks versus the Czarists rule. Even royalty is not immune from the bullet. The assassination of Archduke Franz Ferdinand put President Woodrow Wilson in a precarious predicament. Should the United States enter the global war, or not? The dreaded draft forces me to join the Harlem Hellfighters, or the 369th Infantry Regiment. Black men serve from the entire diaspora: Nigeria, Jamaica, French Guiana, and the USA in World War I under this division. I personally believe that I am above reproach for any conscription because I have a college degree. Afro-American men could not join the Marines; a few serve in the Navy. We are relegated to the US Army. Soldiers sail the Mauritania to reach our final destination: Séchault, France, or the Western Front. The First Battle of Marne proves to be a huge victory for the French because we thwart and avert Hessian strategic attempts from advancing on the Western Front. The Allies literally stop an attack on Paris; after all, the Marne River is simply a tributary of the Seine River. This valley is inspirationally beautiful with its verdant and luxurious greenery for miles, revealing vineyards for the ages. I understand why it has inspired great artists, such as Paul Cézanne. In spite of this, the humiliation of being Negro servicemen is intoxicating.

"How could our military segregate American men premised upon race?" I pondered with the utmost resentment. My only hope and the only positive aspect of this global catastrophe is the rumored *WWI Christmas Truce* in 1914, where German and British troops celebrate this merry season together and halt any bloodshed between us. We serenade one another with carols, share food, and play games in unison in the trenches of Flanders and France. Although, this activity is illicit, I hope this holiday practice becomes a tradition among troops. To my dismay, the years of 1914 and 1918 encounter over 25 million men who would be wounded and die.

Black men are sacrificing our lives daily for our respective countries, yet we are unable to dine, fight, and sleep with our White counterparts. The United States is a dreadful democracy. Our quarters are cramped, and our rifles are confiscated. There are some beautiful men confined with me in our barb wired barracks. I have no idea who is homosexual or straight. My penis is always so hard and erect being around so many handsome male comrades.

I made sure that my jacket covers my groin area, so no one is aware of my secret yearnings. During this dreadful time, I thought solely about Barrington. He mailed a long letter to me stating that his family is going to permanently move to Liberia, West Africa on the S.S. Phyllis Wheatley, one of three of Garvey's shipping cruise liners. I am really happy for them, and my joy emanates from the fact that Barrington escaped the war. Besides the horror of the 'War to end all Wars', as some referred to this mission, people are dying another type of violent death via disease. This killer is coined, 'The Spanish Flu'. This plague did not only enter our infantry, but it spread worldwide. My sister Holly was struck with this curse. She died at Howard University hospital after being admitted for only two days. We never had a chance to say our proper 'goodbyes'. Holly was always kind to everyone, and she never judged me. I wonder if she knew if I am gay. She didn't seem to care about my sexual orientation; alternatively, she was a supportive sibling in every aspect. I miss her more than life itself. I am not sure if I am dreaming, but it is 3:03 a.m. according to my watch. I see a giant glowing orb which resembles a golden bubble. Then, this bubble pokily transmutes into my sister's physical appearance. Holly appears with a very youthful physical body and sits next to me on my bed.

"I love you Peanut. Yes, I always knew that you preferred the same gender that I desired to court. The dead are ubiquitous. It shouldn't matter. Always be true to yourself. I am in such a beautiful dund an amazing place of supreme peace. We can literally see sound here; it has an array of colors and motion. Imagine…the visualization of noise! Hail is an apparition of rainbow waves —steady locomotion of multiple hues. It is difficult to describe the inner joy that I am experiencing. Death is nothing to fear because if everyone knew how truly wonderful this dimension is, there would be mass suicides on a daily basis. Shh, don't tell anyone," Holly laughingly utters.

She told me that I would survive this horrid war, but our parents won't survive the Spanish Influenza which plagues every nation and continent on Earth, except Antarctica. It is highly contagious, and people actually drown in their own fluids. Hospitals are so overrun. Nurses and doctors are absolutely overwhelmed with the number of people being admitted for the Spanish Flu. Unfortunately, there seems to be a 100 percent chance of death for people diagnosed with this rare and frightening disease. Hundreds of corpses are piled outside on sidewalks and alleys surrounding hospitals, homes, and fire stations because the death toll is so high. I feel wretched that I missed Holly's funeral, so I don't want to miss my parents' upcoming funerals. She assures me that I wouldn't. As soon as she appeared, she disappeared, right into thin air. It sounds silly, but I am livid that I forgot to ask her how Mimi and Max are doing on the other side, or fifth dimension. Holly's portent regarding our parents quietuses is only the beginning of things to come.

After a year of clearing ditches from dead bodies, cleaning urine and defecation pails, and fighting the rats inside this excavated Earth for food, the French government finally allows us to use our rifles which the United States withheld from us. My horrific nightmares, which lasted for years long after the war ended, emanate from surviving within the trenches due to the overwhelming stenches. Like my fellow comrades, I would often shroud my body under dead corpses to evade capture from enemy forces afoot. Both the living and the dead are often swathed in shrapnel outlined with crimson from head to toe, mired in soot.

Fellow Colored servicemen chattered about the venomous mutiny within the 24th Infantry Regiment in Houston, Texas primarily based on the fact that Black U.S. soldiers could have arms in France. It is mind-boggling how being an armed black man living in the United States causes so much trepidation from white America. I couldn't stop thinking how accurate Barrington was earlier regarding how all of these trammels of white supremacy are designed to permanently disenfranchise black men. I can't believe that I thought he was extreme with reference to his ideologies. Barrington is right on point!

Living in France, my entire battalion is oblivious to being Black because we are treated with the utmost respect. *Négrophilie* permeates the air like the finest French perfumes infuse a room and entice our senses with the utmost euphoria. *Négrophilie* and the Harlem Renaissance could be interchangeable terms, except white culture in France celebrates black excellence, exactly as Negroes do in New York City. Finally, I am embraced as a fellow human being! French women openly pursue us. Black men could express physical contact with white women in public without any form of retribution by anyone. I never felt so free in my life because I only socialized within my own community circles back in Washington, DC. The culture in France is much more liberal than the United States because they have specific clubs in the open for gay people like me. I met a man who scarily resembled a glamorous and beautiful woman at the Théâtre des Champs-Élysées in

Paris. He prefers to be called by his stage name, Claudette, but his birthname is Claude. Having sex with Claudette is so extraordinary and exhilarating! She would undress privately for me, and it was as if she is on stage performing. My dick is already erect! She removed her top and her chest was hairless, but flat. She had a long and wide cock with curly, thick brown hair crowning it. I got on my knees and sucked her until she ejaculated into my mouth. Then, I fucked her up the ass so hard until I came with cum while she wore sheer red stockings with a seam vertically climbing her hind legs and high heel shoes. I moaned so loudly that I thought the entire neighborhood of Montparnasse in the Left Bank could hear me. This experience is utter ecstasy. I am shocked to learn that Claudette is married with a wife who fully approves of his lifestyle. She would even watch Claudette and I get intimate at times and masturbate to us making love. Antoinette, Claudette's wife, and I would visit museums, cafes and movie shows together. Moreover, no one thought it was odd or strange for whites and blacks to congregate with one another. I had some of the best times in my life with them in Paris. I understand why they call Paris the 'City of Lights', not only due to the wonderful lit edifices, nightclubs, elegantly dressed people, and colorful art, but the luminosity everyone exudes from within and sends it outward to everyone that they meet. Witnessing the Eiffel Tower and promenading along The Avenue des Champs-Élysées, we laughed, drank and listened to some of the best jazz that there is. They are most impressed with my regiment, the 369th and James Reese Europe's band. In spite of all of this hedonistic indulgence, France is strict with the mandate of wearing masks because of this global pandemic: Spanish Influenza. Back home, California is the only state who mandates the wearing of flu masks, and when people don't comply, they could face fines and imprisonment. My befuddlement lies in why some people are resistant to wearing masks when it is a matter of life or death. Millions of people all over the world have already died from this opportunistic plague. Choosing life should always be the first priority for anyone on this planet. By wearing masks, we are not only protecting ourselves, but we are also insulating others from getting sick with our germs. The trenches snake around the French countryside endlessly for miles, concealing venomous men wanting to destroy our enemies at any cost. Fighting in the trenches is one of the worst experiential ordeals anyone could behold because our eyes would avert the scorched earth above us. The rain makes everything worse because the trenches become slippery, and virtually impossible to stand upright without falling down or tripping in the mud. We either meander through walls of dirt, soot, or mud depending on the weather conditions and severity of the battle on any particular day. It is very difficult to detect the direction of gunfire hurling at us. Smoke and residue from the air raids scud across the sky, billowing the land with dark gray fumes carrying a strong miasma of kerosine. The statuesque, verdant trees become burnt cinders; it is such an ungodly sight. Dead bodies pile up like decks of cards, rats rapidly run rampant through the debris; raw sewage supplements the intolerable stench in the trenches; and a constant bombardment of artillery shells and grenades land next to you or your comrade, while another is killed on contact by one. This barrage is unpredictably incessant. So many men are mentally discombobulated due to the aftermath and unpredictability of skirmishing. The worst tussle for me is the large-scale tank offensive at the Battle of Cambrai near Cambrai, France. The use of tank brigades as a fighting tactic offers the ultimate protection for us, but they are bulky and cumbersome. We literally had to remove gigantic tanks out of the trenches. Rarely, when some of these English tanks accidentally collapse into the trenches of Allied forces, a few soldiers were beheaded by the heavy artillery. It is the most gruesome sight for any human being to behold.

The French media, like 'Le Miroir', seldom discusses the negative effects of the Spanish flu because it is too focused on the war. I requested a two-week reintegration from my Captain because I received a correspondence that my father fell ill to the Spanish epidemic. Captain Herbert granted my leave to take a melancholy reprieve back to Washington DC. Entering the hospital room, my father looks so frail and pale. He could barely speak because he couldn't breathe. My mother is always by his side at Howard University hospital. While my dad is still conscious, I told him that I loved him and he was always a great father and husband. He should never worry because I would always look after my mother in his absence. He smiled and tried to nod his head in agreement, but he was too weak. He died the following day. My mother was admitted to the hospital three days after my father's dismal departure. She only lasted one day in the hospital because her symptoms are much more severe than my father's. She had internal bleeding with blood gushing from her nostrils and mouth. All of the dead bodies in France that I buried cannot compare to my return to my beloved homeland and having to bury both of my parents in the ground. I often reminisce about my encounter with Holly in France. I don't feel so bad because I know that death is another doorway to a new paradigm. Our loved ones are renewed. Yet, I do miss them in the physical realm. I am so devastated because my entire nuclear family is decimated by the Spanish influenza. This scourge is a misnomer because it did not emanate from Spain. It most likely started in the U.S. or France. However, Spain is neutral during World War I and never censors its news. Therefore, the Spanish media reports the results and data of this devastating disease of how it sickens and kills people. Because Spain is the only nation reporting specificities of this perilous pandemic, the rest of the world decides to name this killer after Spain. No one is immune from this pandemic, but countries involved in World War I are severely censoring their death toll reporting to prevent looking weak and vulnerable to enemy nations.

It is great to reunite with Barrington and his family at my parent's funeral. Marcus is a handsome teenager, and Meredith has not aged a day since my departure. Heather also attended…clean and sober. She gained a few pounds and carries her extra weight well. I made it quite clear to her that we would never get back together. Cogitatively, I never wanted to be with her in the first place. I only married her to please my parents. Now that they are gone, there is no need to wear a façade. Meredith was kind enough to cater the entire funeral for me. The spread is outstanding. Everyone only removed our face coverings to feast on this excellent repast. Our masks are a striking reminder of the reason for these two funerals. It is amazing how most people are impervious to the sensual, yet subtle glances exchanged between Barrington and I during this fine banquet. Wily casts shared between two parties usually give away surreptitious and intricate relations among people. I am quite apt at detecting this form of nuanced body language because this is a dead giveaway for successfully pursuing and maintaining furtive relationships. She served ham, fried chicken, collard greens, sweet potatoes, cherry pies and chitterlings. I told Barrington about my contact with Holly. He suggested that we conjure my parents via a séance. I vehemently declined out of fear because I did not want them to be aware of my sexual orientation. Barrington professes that if they did not know about you, they know now. I cringe at the thought of it all, but I know in my heart that Barrington is right – he is always sagacious about life in general. I allowed Alma to continue to stay at the residence and earn a salary here. She is so dedicated to our family throughout the years. I directed her to look after my vehicle and use it when it was necessary. Alma also has access to my home, as did Barrington's family until I permanently returned to the United States. My childhood home is spotless and pristine, just how I remembered it. I wasn't sure if I was going to eventually sell my parents' home or not. I have two days before I had to deploy back to France. Spending time with my close friends back home is a surreal emprise for me. Barrington and I were able to sneak one rendezvous before my deployment. He changed because our love making seemed quick, cold, and mechanical. We did not French kiss, face one another by grinding or cuddle in bed. He spread my buttocks and butt plugged me until he came. Then, he pushed my head down to suck his dick. He hastily pulled his boxer briefs and pants up and rushed away from me. I did not complain, but my anus is so sore and burns similarly to when I have constant diarrhea for hours on end. Luckily for me, there is no blood streaming from it. He whispered that he'll be in touch. I certainly did not feel any love from him; I was too afraid to infer if our relationship is in jeopardy. Now our love making is nothing short of presumptuous hostility. A doom of loneliness drapes itself around me. The city looked so splendid with the sun shining, beautiful architecture intact, and the blooming of cherry blossom trees slowly frolicking along the Potomac River. The sun reflects its brilliant orange image like a virulent fire just beneath the water's surface.

We fought about 115 miles east of Paris, and thanks to the altruistic French government, we are confident to combat the Germans with our French Lebel rifles. We often hull injured and dying soldiers to the tents to be treated by military doctors and nurses from the American Red Cross. When it rains, the trenches would usually fill with mud approximately two feet in height. I often witness the medical staff sawing off limbs to prevent gangrene, dressing burn wounds and removing bullets and shrapnel. Wistfully, dying men lie lifeless on their beds with their eyes wide open staring blankly into space. We wore masks and eye goggles not just for the Spanish Influenza, but to avoid breathing bomb residue, mustard gas, dust, and dirt in the trenches. Oddly, some areas of the ditches are deserted. I notice that two French soldiers are arguing. I didn't understand exactly what they are saying because my French is so rudimentary. However, I tried to defuse the situation, as best as I could. When they saw me, they immediately smiled and thanked me for my service. Hence, the French greatly appreciate the help that the United States provides them to defeat Germany. We made our introductions. The tall, dark one is named, Pierre, while the stout blonde is called Jacques. I found both of these men to be very handsome. We trudged back to our designated quarters, which is about an hour one way always being vigilant not to get pummeled by an air missile. Not to mention the German Zeppelin airships strategically aiming their missiles into our trenches with the ghastly smell of mustard gas which is so unnerving and perturbing, it enabled many of us to lose our ability to sleep. Their incessant stares signaled that they might be gay. I wasn't sure, so I played it cool. Pierre and Jacques share a tent together. They asked in the worst-sounding English that I have ever heard, if I wanted to join them for some authentic French treats. I enthusiastically concurred. I dined on authentic French cuisine: Château Clos Haut-Peyraguey 1917, buttered and garlic infused escargot and camembert cheese. I never drank heated wine; it is delectable. Pierre and Jacques are ingenious for warming the wine inside the front-line trench to aid in keeping us from not freezing to death. This elegant meal is so nostalgic because it took me back to the repast at my parent's funeral. As I pondered on my life and the abrupt changes transpiring, I realize that Washington DC and Paris are similar cities. The most similar characteristic is that both of them are built in a geometric circle; the street grids are almost identical. This coincidence did not happen by happenstance because Washington, DC was designed by the French architect: Pierre L'Enfant. I want to visit the Père

Lachaise Cemetery alone to commune with Holly. It is filled with intense pink cherry blossom trees. I don't know why, but I feel very at ease with sharing my sexual orientation to Pierre and Jacques. They giggled and admitted that they already knew. I was shocked and perplexed. Yet, my overall fear is to be reviled for being gay. "It is verdi common en France and you have zhee noticeable traits," they simultaneously announced with huge grins. "We are not judshing you in any way because en France you can be free to be who you really want to be," they stated. I shook my head agreeing with them in complete silence. Like the living and the dead portals, everything is vibrational. Serendipitously, these two men were born and raised in Alsace, France, but relocated to Paris. They are both Jewish. Their families had to vacate the Alsace-Lorraine region due to fear of German occupation during WWI. Pierre's eldest brother is a rich banker and famous photographer, Albert Khan. Pierre shared beautiful photographs with us taken from all over the world in color. I never saw such gorgeous portraits that mimicked life instead of appearing only in black and white. Khan's stellar images are like looking into an actual mirror. Finally, they introduced me to other gay men in our battalion. Luckily, I had an all-night watch with another gay soldier. I remember him from the group of homosexuals that Khan pointed out to me. We were isolated in a trench far from other soldiers. We approached No-Man's Land, which is quite risky, but we wanted to remain undetected. We put our rifles down and tongued one another. He rubbed his hands on my butt and pulled my fishtail pants down. We grind naked and then we give fellatio simultaneously to one another until we both came in each other's mouths. Finally, he throws my body facing the muddy ground and fucks me up the ass with the utmost intense passion. My entire body could not stop shaking from the stimulating exhilaration. His sperm explodes and billows inside of my anus feeling like viscous and warm whipped cream. Not to mention that his cum tastes so sweet. I felt ecstasy from the top of my head to the tip of my toes. We are startled by a slight noise we hear and quickly get dressed. We didn't even bother to exchange names. But I will never forget his face should we have another sexual encounter.

Pierre is a hero; he is certainly no narcissist because he never breathed a word of his heroics himself. It is rumored that he was instrumental with the strategic planning of the killing of the infamous Prussian 'The Red Baron': Manfred von Richthofen. The year is 1918 and airplanes exist. I never really conceived that the Wright Brothers would successfully invent a flying machine because it seemed like a notion of fantasy at the time. They are similar to automobiles, but they have wings and propellers to keep them suspended in the air. I wonder what birds think when they see airplanes because they resemble gawky, metal flying fowl. It is simply mind-boggling and mesmerizing to experience all of the amazing inventions made during these last two decades. The Red Baron has a sporty, red airplane that shot down around 80 Allied aircraft. He is a formidable enemy; his deadly precision never misses enemy fighter pilots, which earned him another nickname: 'flying ace'. Anti-German sentiment resonates and permeates throughout the United States. Because of the war, President Woodrow Wilson's infamous 1917 Flag Day speech fueled the flames to scorch and burn the reputation of innocent Germans residing within the United States. President Wilson forces German Americans to sign a registration affidavit, falsely admitting that they are 'alien enemies'. Thus, German Americans suffer from a cloud of suspicion, causing them to be admitted into government internment facilities throughout the United States. Racial discrimination always seems to victimize foreign nationals residing within the United States. The Germans' only crime is their ethnicity.

Wearing masks is still customary in France due to the Spanish Flu. Millions are still dying from this plague and the war. This epoch is the great human purge due to the multitude of deaths incessantly happening worldwide. With the exception of my immediate family, the exponential toll of demise on Earth is starting to numb my soul. I lost hearing in my right ear due to the constant barrage of grenades and bombs being dropped from the air. I consider myself lucky because I have my eyesight intact and all of my limbs. So many of my comrades have died or been maimed from this dreadful war. The saddest travesty of all is that some soldiers no longer have a grasp of reality. The pressure of fighting, slaughter and destruction caused them to lose their minds entirely. It is November 11th, and it is extremely cold. We heard word that Germany is about to sign an Armistice. Ironically, General John Pershing forced Americans to continue to fight. Over 3,500 U.S. soldiers still sacrificed their lives when the fighting should have ceased. French citizens shower fallen soldiers equally, both Negro and White battalions with red poppy flowers. Upon returning to the United States, Pershing faced a

Congressional hearing to explain why he made soldiers engage in combat when he knew about the armistice in advance. The homecoming is very different for Black and White veterans. The French are the first to award our regiment with the Croix de Guerre medal. Our selfless service, sacrifice and heroism are confronted with pervasive racism, carnage and hostility. Many Whites attempt to cleave our confidence upon our homecoming with their unabating dehumanization towards us. Most Afro-Americans extol me for my service, yet I receive dirty looks from many Euro-Americans, especially when I wear my uniform. My brethren to the South are not as fortunate, as I. Many of these fine soldiers are lynched, publicly humiliated and disfigured for simply being Black World War I veterans. To make matters worse, many never received a red cent in pension for their military service. I am so grateful that my family left me a substantial inheritance because my veteran's administration benefits took an entire year to disburse. My hearing in my right ear eventually restored itself, yet I experience the worst nightmares that would jolt me from my deepest slumber. I would drink heated milk to get me to fall back to sleep again. I keep close contact via letters and telephone calls with Claudette and his wife, Antoinette, on a monthly basis. I also keep in touch with Pierre Khan twice a year. He is quite wealthy because he resides in the Jewish neighborhood coined the 9th arrondissement. Pierre is an echt Frenchman: he wears elegant clothing, speaks with the perfect accent and displays a demure attitude. Pierre sends me astonishing polychrome pictures of the pyramids of Giza in Egypt, The Great Wall of China, Jasper Park, Canada, Bombay, India and Kyoto,

Japan. His brother's images exude life with the vivid colors in real time, as opposed to the customary Black and White photographs which depict death. These pictures inspire me to plan future trips to Africa and Asia. Albert's photographic prowess is done in an anthropological way, displaying the commonalties of global culture. His artistic style envelops a very uniting methodology. I am edified that native Egyptians are Black and look just like Afro-Americans. I have a profound understanding why Napoleon Bonaparte shot off the noses of the Egyptian Sphinx and other Egyptian statues because he refused to accept that Negros could be instrumental with creating and sustaining such an intricate and powerful historical society. I often think about Barrington and wonder if he and his family made it to Liberia.

Regardless of how cold it is, signages advise the public to keep our bedroom windows open in order to prevent catching the Spanish Flu. My parents' home has white cast-iron steam radiators on each floor. The heat emitted from each steam radiator is so potent that it blocked the chill from the cold air flowing from outside through the windows. We do not dare to touch steam radiators with our bare hands because third degree burns are sure to ensue! Statuesque steam radiators situated alongside our windows are our best defense to eradicate this infinitesimal murderer because we are able to inhale fresh air. Time always reveals revelations. The cracked and peeling white paint hanging amid the three steam radiators on each floor divulge their harden gray and dismal interiors. They beseech a much-needed paint job. The United States is ridiculous for politicizing the wearing of masks or not. Unlike the United States, France has no issue with saving lives. Newspapers print instructions for how people could even make their own masks at home. People who are noncompliant face prison time, fines or having their name published in the paper, revealing they are a 'mask slacker'. Many schools, churches, and saloons are closed in the United States. We are reminded daily not to cough or sneeze in someone's face. The U.S. media constantly tells us to avoid large events or hold them outside whenever possible. Last, but not least, no spitting of any kind because saliva kills. Health and city officials disseminate these guidelines in a myriad of ways. In Philadelphia, streetcar signs warn, 'Spit Spreads Death'. In New York City, officials enforce no-spitting ordinances and encourage residents to cough or sneeze into handkerchiefs. The city's health department even advises people not to kiss, except through a handkerchief. Even the national wire espouses this same message nationwide. Another natural disaster is the 1906 Earthquake in San Francisco, that climaxed to almost eight on the Richter scale, causing a massive fire killing over 3,000 residents. Promisingly, flu cases in San Francisco declined in early November 1918. After the armistice on November 11, San Francisco ended its mask order. Naturally, a spike in flu cases occurred in January 1919 which led the city to implement a second masking mandate, but this one faced more resistance. Around the same time the San Francisco Chronicle ran its mask public service announcements, newspapers around the country published a cartoon of a man hacking horrendously in public that warned, "Coughs and Sneezes Spread Diseases: As Dangerous As Poison Gas Shells"— again linking battling the flu to fighting in World War I.

This particular campaign incenses me to no end! Yes, the Spanish Flu is deadly, but I avow that our service in the Army is trivialized with this ill-equipped analogy. Yes, wearing a mask is taxing and it is difficult to breathe, but if it saves lives, I still don't see what the problem is. Newspapers use the cartoon to illustrate coverage of a special bulletin from Surgeon General, Rupert Blue about the Spanish flu and how U.S. citizens could protect ourselves from it. Although, most people comply with the mask ordinances, some people claim that they are an infringement upon their civil liberties. Some people try to cut corners regarding the mask guidelines by poking holes in their masks to smoke cigarettes. Cities that passed masking mandates in the fall of 1918 struggled to enforce them among the small portion of people who rebelled. In one dreadful incident in San Francisco, a special officer for the board of health shot a man who refused to wear a mask as well as two other bystanders…the saga of violence perdures.

Boy oh boy…it is liken to being clobbered in the head with a 2 by 4 living in the United States. The War to end all wars is officially over, and innocent people are still mercilessly dying because of narcissistic and hedonistic tendencies. Just wear a fucking mask! The only protections the international public have are social distancing and the wearing of face coverings because they are no elixirs, cures, or medicines to protect us. I sold my rowhouse and moved into my parents' spectacular building. I garnished a pretty penny for my property, almost doubled than what I paid for it initially. I could comfortably afford Alma remaining at my parents' residence carrying on with her household duties. I miss my parents and Holly so much, especially moving back into my childhood abode. Holly never married or had children; however, she was very fulfilled with her life. She adored books, so that is why I think that she became a librarian. According to Barrington, the three of them are enjoying life in another paradigm together. Heather keeps coming around to visit me. I suppose she wants to keep our marriage intact. She quit drinking, but I still prefer to be alone or spend time with Barrington. I gave Heather an ultimatum, which is we will only have anal and oral sex together, if she wants to remain living with me. Her character is so feeble that she agreed to my domestic terms and sexual contingencies. I finally received communications from Barrington. He telephoned me with the most dreadful news. Hoover had sabotaged their ship to sail to Liberia by planting Afro-American FBI agents to damage Garvey's ship. This predicament is almost impossible to prove, but everyone knows that Hoover is behind this doomed destination. His only objective is to usurp Garvey. Due to Hoover's plotting and scheming, Garvey ended up in prison because of trumped up charges. Thus, Barrington decides to rent out his home in Georgetown and buy another Brownstone in Harlem to be closer to Garvey and his mission. He briefed me that he would be returning to DC to finalize any last-minute moving provisions. He wants me to keep an eye on his new tenants because they are elderly. He knows them well, so there is no need to vet them. They are members of his family's ritualistic séances. These two sisters, in their sixties, are renting Barrington's place.

Providentially, Barrington, Meredith, and Marcus are healthy and alive. Meredith becomes a casualty of Barrington's philandering. Meredith's micturitions are coupled with severe pain, like a burning, stinging inferno. Meredith is exceedingly chaste, so she had to have contracted gonorrhea, or clap, from her husband. She was treated with Silver proteinate. Ironically, Barrington did not have clap. However, he assumed that she must have caught it from him due to his homosexual affairs. Barrington is a chauvinist at best because he never saw his wife's obsession with female prostitutes. Meredith had at least six trysts with courtesans in Harlem. She met these working women at night clubs or movie houses during the height of the Harlem Renaissance, when they lived on 135th Street and 5th Avenue. The Widgeons cohabitate along Lenox Avenue, where chic temptations abound everywhere within walking distance. This era delineates the Black mecca (Harlem) in America for Afro-American cultural excellence. Harlem blossoms and blooms with ebony writers, businessmen, entertainers, doctors, educators and social activists. It is a place denoting the African-diaspora with the utmost pride and dignity. To my surprise, Meredith and Barrington married one another to compensate and conceal both of their homosexual tendencies. It was the perfect marriage of convenience to keep their lifestyles furtive and private against peering eyes from those not in the know. I wondered if Pierre and Claudette would be able to discern Meredith's bisexual tendencies. She certainly fooled me because she always exudes femininity, coyness, and elegance. I don't understand why Barrington would keep their relationship status a secret from me. Although, he eventually disclosed these vital particulars to me. I am afraid to question his coldness regarding our last sexual contact together, but I ask anyway.

"I resent you and your privileged life of entitlement, Peanut," he explained.

"I am not the one who is entitled because I literally fought in World War I!" I screamed to the top of my lungs. "I don't recall you sacrificing your life overseas for any battles of late!"

"Let me stop you right here, Hunter. First of all, I am referring to you and your family's fair complexions!" Barrington scolded.

Barrington only refers to me as Hunter when he is upset.

"I can't control my physical appearance, Barrington!"

"True, but you can constrain all of the advantageous opportunities presented to you because of your light-skin when your brothers and sisters of a darker hue get overlooked for jobs, housing, university matriculation, and political advancement to name a few entitlements," he scolded. "Whites partially accept mulattoes because you reflect their narcissism by resembling their race. They will never fully accept you due to our One Drop rule in the United States," Barrington affirmed.

"They are genetic mutations of us. Pure and simple," Barrington insisted.

"If this is the case, then why do they control the world as we know it?" I exasperatedly queried.

"This ownership is and will be short-lived in comparison to other cultures worldwide. Hence, it has only been for about 500 years." Barrington took a 30-second pause before he said 500 years. "In the days of Yore, Kemet rulers of Egypt, or Pharaonic royalty, controlled their dynasties for millennia before the Arab invasions. Also, the demonym of Australia had sovereignty over their land for over 40,000 years before the English arrived. It is simply a matter of perspective," Barrington proclaims. "Their constant fear and obsession with becoming a global minority galvanizes their insidiousness towards Colored races on the planet and the Earth itself. They deem that they must have dominion over people unlike them, both animate and inanimate organisms and the entire universe."

"The entire universe, seriously?" I voice in confusion.

"Absolutely, the whole cosmos: asteroids, forests, fish, the weather, mountains, oceans and etcetera." Barrington scoffs while laughing.

"That would be a gigantic white ethnostate." I chuckled in a loud outburst.

Whenever I make direct eye-contact with Barrington, an electric pulse rushes from the top of my head, trailing directly through my heart warming my entire body. It is pure love that I have for him. I am still bashful whenever I look at him directly because my natural reaction is just to look away. I believe that my feelings for him are more intense and profound than his sentiments are for me. Relationships always seem to have a weaker partner. Heather is and has always been weak for me. I guess it is just a part of life. I never consciously thought that I was superior to Barrington because of my coloring; alternatively, I am madly in love with him. I can comprehend that his notions on white supremacy are not gibberish, but I still find them to be extreme. Again, I am not raised in the deep South because Washington, DC is located in the MidAtlantic region of the United States. Furthermore, I am never intimate with whites. My father used to go to certain 'White Only' establishments to buy us the best merchandise because he could pass as them. He never befriended members of their race because his purpose is to solely use them for what he needed when it was convenient for him. I am so ecstatic because I bought a train ticket to visit Barrington and his family in Harlem.

A few weeks after my birthday, the Volstead Act, or Eighteenth Amendment, passed, and Prohibition is official. Heather is about to lose her mind. She worried about this mandate all year long, and it has finally manifested itself. 'The Jazz Age', or the Roaring Twenties, begins with a bang! I got used to having Heather around because I could have all of the anal sex with her as I pleased. She frequently gives me blow jobs, so I guess one could say that we are happily married.

Though this year is very sobering, women finally attain the right to vote with the passing of the 19th Amendment! Thus, 1920 is going to be a year of dichotomies. Heather has and will always have a penchant towards soporific substances. I did not learn until it was too late that Heather is addicted to laudanum. Her moods are very different compared to when she drank gin. She sleeps for hours on end; I assumed that she was simply fatigued most of the time. I left her at home when I went to visit Barrington in Harlem. Setting eyes on Barrington always makes my penis erect. I could not wait for him to caress my entire body with his strong, soft hands and cuddle with him in his bed. Meredith had taken Marcus to his violin lesson, then to his friend's house for dinner for a few hours. The exterior of

Barrington's home boasted a Beaux-Arts architectural style. When I arrived at their luxurious brownstone, as soon as I entered his residence, he embraced me by grabbing my buttocks really tight and we tongue-kissed for about five minutes, but it felt like an eternity. My heart races and my breathing is so deep. As we canoodle, we grind so intensely that I ejaculate inside my trousers. Finally, we undress while straddling each other's legs ever so tightly in an interlocked position. Barrington sucked my dick to get me hard again and I had an orgasm inside of his mouth. Later, I rode him doggy style… I could not get enough of him. My toes tightly clenched as my bodily sensations peaked the ultimate crescendo. I love to hear Barrington's jagged, heavy breathing when we make love to one another because I interpret it as Barrington is reaching his maximum climax. Sometimes, our love making is so synchronized that we will climax simultaneously. Hence, this experience is nothing short of a fireworks explosion. In the heat of the moment, I would give Barrington fellatio before he was able to bathe or shower because I relished the aroma of his sour smelling sweaty balls. I am addicted to his pheromones. We went to town on one another; I always preferred to kiss and cuddle with Barrington unlike the other men that I fucked. Luckily, Barrington did not contract the clap from Meredith because he only had sex with her when her soars weren't visible. Most importantly, her medication does a good job of eradicating her disease. The only times that I sense wholeness is being with Barrington. They have a huge porcelain bathtub where Barrington and I bathe comfortably together. We interdigitate one another for a final time inside the lukewarm water. We donned our clothing as quickly as we possibly could. Fully dressed, we sat in his library and wait for Meredith and Marcus' return while playing chess and listening to 'Nobody' on his record player. We greeted each other with hugs. Marcus is a splitting image of Barrington; he's changed so much since I was in the war. Meredith prepared a feast, as usual. Her fine cooking took me back to my parents' repast.

"Are you still conducting frequent séances?" I inquired.

The three of them smirked at me and remained silent. Meredith broke the stoic silence by laughing about our experience with Mimi and Max.

"Do you own any pets?" she asked.

"Besides, Heather, you mean? No, I don't have any four-legged family members at this time," I replied, giggling.

My, how times have changed! Barrington hired an immigrant Irish female maid named Fiona. Their home was exquisite and adorned with the most exotic art that I have ever seen. The entire abode is decorated with the latest upholsteries. Chesterfield furniture enriches the living and dining rooms crowned with built-in celestial tin ceilings. An ebony-carved head of Akhenaton, a tapestry depicting Harriet Tubman, and a humungous oil painting of Toussaint L'Ouverture victorious in Haiti hangs in their living room, with verdant ferns potted inside pendulous copper pots.

Barrington is friendly with 'Queenie', or Stephanie St. Clair who, in her own right independently and successfully owns and operates several Negro banks exclusively serving Black people throughout the entire Harlem community. They were personally introduced by Garvey, and Barrington owes his financial solvency to St. Clair. Thus,

St. Clair and Garvey both come from the Caribbean islands, or the West Indies. St. Clair disdains the European diaspora, so Barrington would act as a go-between for Al Capone's money by laundering it without her knowledge. This is the only deceptive action that Barrington hides from her. In any event, they profited greatly from Capone's investments. St. Clair's glistening and deeply dark hue shimmers like chocolate pudding silhouetting a muscular, yet thin tapestry from head to toe. St. Clair is indifferent of how Negroes earn their income, whether by lawful or unlawful means. She always launders money to Barrington when he does not want his financial transactions to be traced by any federally owned banks. Harlem has thriving Black owned banks. Stephanie, without hesitation, loaned Barrington $20,000 dollars to bail out one of Garvey's shipping businesses. St. Clair is a lone businesswoman and heroine who willingly defends her turf and assets by any means necessary. First and foremost, St. Clair is shrouded in mystery. She shoots to kill! In spite of her criminal ruthlessness and business savvy, she always exudes dignity via her fashionable attire and lavish lifestyle. She loathes white supremacy at any level, and she is always determined to undermine this racist regime destroying the African diaspora living throughout the United States, particularly via law enforcement. Most Whites who encounter St. Clair are very intimidated by her surly presence. They perceive her to be arrogant because she emits so much self-love for herself, her community, and her heritage. She emanates from the nation of Guadalupe which explains her thick French accent. St. Clair donated the beautiful portrait of Haiti's freedom fighter, Toussaint L'Ouverture, to Barrington's family. St. Clair keenly observes that most Afro-Americans display a modicum of subservience when confronting their White counterparts. However, she astutely witnesses that Barrington consistently approaches European-Americans with vitriol, vehemence, and pride. Stephanie declares that Barrington must be Caribbean, like herself, due to these particular display of behaviors. Barrington and St. Clair protect one another by watching each other's backs with the tremendous treachery that abounds in Harlem. St. Clair is another shining example that women deserve the same rights as men. Barrington always has multiple sources of income due to his loyalty and immense integrity. He never drops a dime on his friends and family.

They have a mahogany staircase spiraling in both directions and mahogany paneling inlaid with ebony. Their entire flooring is comprised of white marble. Crystal chandeliers illuminate from high ceilings, announcing their wealth in his library. Most of his repertoire of books are by authors of the African diaspora, but he shared one text with me to saliently stipulate Garvey's movement. It is entitled, 'The Rising Tide of Color: The Threat Against White World-Supremacy' by Lothrop Stoddard. Barrington's discourse professes that since colonization and slavery of people of color, Europeans have been obsessed with genetic annihilation of their race from non-white people around the world. Whenever Caucasians witness non-whites, they observe their disappearance. Ironically, Whites do not feel superior to us because they indelibly fear that our melanization will wipe out their ethnic corporeality on a global scale. Thus, exponential race mixing will be the bane of their existence. This core credo creates and continues to perpetuate and catalyze their suppressive and subversive laws, hostile violence, and depraved demeanors towards non-European populations. The recent debacle with Reconstruction is a prime example. Who knew…Whites are jealous of our melanin. Moreover, they attest to obsessing, loathing, and agonizing over a brown and black-dominated planet. I looked forward to reading this particular piece of literature when I return to Georgetown. On my final day with the Widgeons, we visited a notorious speakeasy owned by our people called Queen Nzinga. Most Coloreds are making significant progress, such as the gorgeous actress Anna May Wong who is the first Asian-American to appear on U.S. currency.

We are not heavy drinkers, although, we do drink socially. I might indulge in a sip of wine or two. Their main objective is for me to witness the plentitude of contraband alcohol that is still available, along with the multitude of inebriated patrons, in spite of the new law. Unbeknownst to me, Holly attended some of Barrington's weekly séances revealing future tragedies coming my way. Holly enjoined Barrington to warn me in order to prevent such dreadful forthcoming events.

Chapter 3
"Scarborough Fair/Canticle"
by Simon & Garfunkel

The train ride from Harlem is terrific, in spite of my overwhelming fatigue. Although my trip to New York City was swell, as a caveat, I am glad to be back in the District of Columbia because its energy is much more serene and pristine in comparison to Harlem. I can see the cherry blossom trees in the distance from all panoramas on the train. I knocked on the door, and Heather did not answer, so I opened it with my key. When I arrived upstairs to our bedroom, she is sprawled on the bed facing downward on her stomach. I see a phial on the floor right under her right hand. When I picked it up in order to examine the small print, it reads laudanum. It is too late to call the pharmacy for help because it is closed, so I shook Heather as hard as I could attempting to wake her. Five minutes later, which seemed like an eternity, she finally gains consciousness.

"Why are you drinking laudanum?" I angrily asked.

"I feel so down and depressed all of the time," Heather coyly replied. "You should hear the dreadful and daunting discourse shared with me by many European-Americans," Heather added.

"What do you mean?" I said forcefully.

"Last Tuesday, I went to the bank to cash a check. Well, you won't believe what this white female teller said to me!"

"Do tell," I retorted with sarcasm.

"You don't need to show any identification. This procedure is for Niggers and other darkies," she saliently stipulated.

"I was silent and smiled," Heather responded sobbing.

"I am so ashamed, but I was helpless for not defending our race. You know that I could have gotten in big trouble for being inside a 'white Only' establishment, if they knew that I was colored," she rationalized.

Sadly, many people are not curing our deep-rooted issues because we continue to bury them with superficial stints of hedonism. Thus, Heather replaces other unhealthy practices for her drinking addiction.

Heather recalls other incidents of a few Whites making derogatory comments in front of her about Black people because they think that she is also Caucasian. These dreadful and deplorable statements are too much for her to bear. Her reactions to these dehumanizing insults remind me of a term coined by Barrington called, 'White Frailty'. She retorted that some Euro-Americans mock the numerous Afro-Americans lynched throughout the South and wish that all Blacks are exterminated, like cockroaches. Their hope is that our planet would be rid of us once and for all. I tried to reassure Heather that their discrimination is not her fault and she should read Stoddard's novel with me to understand the underpinnings of White Supremacy on a global scale.

"Who is Stoddard?" she responded with a frown.

"Barrington loaned his book to me. He is a Caucasian man delineating the deep-rooted nuances of racism," I clearly clarified.

"I don't enjoy reading books, Peanut. I'd rather sneak away to one of the many speakeasys in town," she chuckled.

"I should have known that you would inevitably find out about the local illicit drinking holes," I sneered.

"Peanut, please. Can we go and visit one? I haven't had a drink in months," Heather pleaded.

"I have a confession to make. The Widgeons and I attended a speakeasy in Harlem. It was amazing! Beautiful, educated, classy, sexy, and wealthy Black people abound while dancing and frolicking all night long," I rejoiced.

I was so aroused reminiscing about my experience in Harlem that I forcefully and aggressively tongue-kissed Heather; we actually made love. I viscerally knew that taking Heather to a speakeasy was wrong, but a part of me wanted her to be happy. Barrington called me and alerted me to the fact that Meredith caught the clap from Fiona. Who knew there is a live-in lover right under his nose? Barrington admitted that he was a tad bit jealous, yet he couldn't be a hypocrite because of me. Oddly, Barrington has not been with any other man sexually besides me. On the contrary, he cheats with a lot of women. His housekeeper, Fiona is no exception.

The nation's capital is hit hardest with Prohibition because our saloons and liquor sales ceased in 1917 due to the Sheppard Bone-Dry Act. Harlem is not the only place to quaff great booze and caper to the best jazz, as Washington, DC, has the Krazy Kat Klub and Throck's Studio. I really relish this particular den of vice because it openly embraces homosexuals. Entering speakeasys is an intricate process. One needs to master patience and passwords because the FBI is always looking to raid, arrest, and permanently discontinue the business of moonshine. Unlike the nation's capital, Harlem's speakeasys are primarily occupied by Afro-Americans, with a few Euro-Americans scattered here and there.

Miraculously, the Spanish influenza ended in April of last year. No one knows why or how, it just did. For three years, we masqueraded around the world disguised. It is a weird sensation going out in public without wearing masks because we seem naked. It is Saturday night on the eve of my 32nd birthday, so Heather and I decided to carouse at Krazy Kat. Heather really dresses well and is exceedingly striking. She wears white sheer stockings with a seem vertically running on her back legs, a pink fringe dress and gold Mary Janes. Heather refuses to cut her hair for any fashion trend. She has to pin her hair up because it is so long in order to wear her golden chiffon Cloche hat. Her hair reaches the tip of her lower back. Whenever she wears a Cloche, it accentuates her striking beauty by highlighting her chiseled facial features. I didn't look too shabby myself, because I sport a cream wool flat cap, two-tone beige and brown Oxford shoes, and a dark brown zoot suit.

"Peanut, you look dashing!" Heather proudly proclaimed.

I simply returned her compliment with a genuine smile. My goal is to watch revelers dance to jazz music until the early morning hours in order to forget the horrors of war which plague me almost nightly. We waited for two hours and had to know a series of coded language before we were allowed inside. Once we enter this magical portal, all of our worries seem to dissipate. It is dimly lit, but the music is loud. Liquor, perfume, and cigarette smoke simultaneously waft through the air, and engulf this venue like children inside of a candy store. However, the redolence of juniper berries dominates because gin is always a win during Prohibition. People are intimately conversing, smoking and dancing the 'Charleston'. Amazingly, I notice homosexuals openly expressing affection for one another; this applies to both men and women. It is so rare to witness such acts within the protestant religiosity heralded upon the United States of America. However, this nightclub scene resonates with Parisian etiquette. I am transfixed as Heather ingests her first sip of moonshine; my stomach has butterflies. It is as if a demonic fluidity possesses her soul. After three drinks and an entire hour, she licks her lips indulgently, clears her throat to conceal her slurred verbiage, while her eyes transform from welcoming amicability into rageful hostility. I thought to myself that this is going to be a warzone, so I better keep away from her crossfires. Heather's foul lexicon has the precision of a German torpedo which triggers people's reactions, yet the repercussions are more devastating. I hope that the acoustics will drown out any profanities emanating from Heather tonight. I am planning on having a good time, as opposed to being bombarded with Heather's humiliation. There was nothing anyone could do to dulcify Heather's pugnacious persona of intoxication. To my surprise, the irate look within Heather's eyes is raging lust for me. She grabs me by the hand and tongue-kissed me. Then, shockingly, she finally leads me into the women's bathroom. She shut and locks the door and performs fellatio on me until I come onto her face. She swallows as much of my sperm as she could. Heather strikingly reminds me of Claudette in Paris. I instruct her to pull her panties down to her ankles, just so I could look closely at her physique. Heather has a natural hour-glass figure. Her brown, frizzy pubic hair augments her creamy hue. We fuck standing upright, facing one another. We have sex again in the restroom stall like two rabbits in heat. She screams to the top of her lungs before it is all over, said and done. Some impatient patrons bang on the door, so that is our cue to rapidly vacate the premises.

"Get a room, why don't you?" a drunken White woman shouted.

Heather has a look of rage, so I put my arms around her to assuage her to walk in the opposite direction in order to prevent a scene. My touch is enough because Heather turns to me with a smile and suddenly almost falls asleep while walking. I catch her and carry her to a table and chair. I propped her body to sit upward so she would inconspicuously appear awake. As I look around, there are so many other inebriated customers, no one really pays any attention to Heather. Because of the ill-repute nature of speakeasies, they are exceedingly integrated in terms of race. One can find both coloreds and whites hobnobbing within the same establishment. This kind of atmosphere reminds me of France. We stayed at the Kat until 6 a.m. so, Heather could remain asleep. She eventually regains advertency and she is able to walk. We drive home in our new Ford Model T, which is the same color as our first one: green.

We arrive home safely and without any drama. Heather is extremely hung over, so she went straight to bed. Our telephone rang, and I think to myself that it is too early (6:30 a.m.) to receive calls. Antionette is on the line sobbing because Claudette had succumbed to complications resulting from the Spanish Flu yesterday. I understood that she was really ill in March of last year, but everyone assumed that she would recover since she was eating, walking, and back to normal activities. Unfortunately, her lung capacity drastically deteriorated. Ironically, more people perished to the Spanish flu than World War One. Millions perished from this disease worldwide. I am melancholy because I will not be able to physically be present at Claudette's funeral. It is so strange that I just thought about her last night. I sent money, accompanied with a colored photograph given to me by Pierre of the Eiffel Tower, to Antoinette to pay my respects. Death intertwines, introduces, dances, and toils itself around me numerous times during this past decade. We have grown accustomed to one another and become very close acquaintances. Thanks to Barrington's séances, I am at ease with my friend's transition because of my close encounters with Holly, Mimi, and Max. Unlike the latter, I have no interest on conducting séances for my parents or Claudette. I appreciated them in the living; however, I set boundaries with them now.

Alma prepared a breakfast fit for a king. She cooked buttered grits, baked a ham with the bone in, scrambled eggs, fried potatoes, biscuits with gravy, and fried cinnamon apples. Heather is in no condition to eat, so I enjoyed this magnificent feast to myself. She is so hungover that she slumbered the entire day. Her entire body reeks of a brewery. I surmised that the smell emanated from her pores. Prohibition signages are strewn everywhere inside the city and throughout the United States. They read, "Outlawed or Legalized…Alcohol is Poison," pictured with a skull juxtaposed with a red background simulating blood. Heather rouses by vomiting. Without uttering a word, she used our Chesterfield couch as her doss for the remainder of the day. She didn't even bother to brush her teeth or bathe. Meredith still plays the harp and sings spiritual hymns for famous black celebrities. She even invited Ida B. Wells to their home to play her one of Fisk's famous ballads: 'Swing Low Sweet Chariot', and discuss the hypocrisy of the suffrage movement by white women. Meredith invited 15 members from Garvey's organization to try to mobilize White women to acknowledge the perils of lynching. Unfortunately, not one member of the National American Women Suffrage Association (NAWSA) accepted Meredith's invitation to attend this mini conference on women's rights. NAWSA deeply discriminated against women of color, particularly African Americans and Chinese. It is monumental that women have the right to vote, but ignoring White supremacist atrocities against Coloreds is a travesty that needs to be addressed and resolved. The NAACP and UNIA join forces to put pressure on the suffrage movement and assuage them to acknowledge the crazed carnage assaulting Afro-Americans in the United States of America. I mention this fact to Heather about the comradery between the Widgeon family and Ida B. Wells, but she exudes total indifference. Heather is so preoccupied with staring into space or outside of our windows. She refuses to engage in conversation; she barely eats or keeps in touch with her family. I apprised our local pharmacy to prohibit selling her anymore laudanum; however, Heather is very clever. She orders vials from the Sears and Roebuck catalog. Barrington and Meredith continue to fight White Supremacy; nevertheless, they immerse in erotic threesomes with Fiona. Their hypocrisy lies with their proclivity for having venereal intimacies with whites.

Pierre called me just to see how I am doing. He is always so genuinely thoughtful. He mentions how is brother Albert commissions female photographers to help change the world by photographing foreign places in color. This photographic methodology enables people to observe other places as part of humanity instead of denigrating overseas cultures, which leads to xenophobia. Because of the suffrage movement, he wants to promote and encourage more women to equally participate in the workforce. Pierre predicts that colored photos will be normalized in the future, much like airplanes are now.

"How can polychrome pictures change the world?" I insisted.

"Albert viscerally deduces that viewing people this way makes them real and tangible. Thus, they cannot be objectified. These connections help unite our planet due to our perceived commonalties, as opposed to fearing one another premised upon our salient superficialities," Pierre professed.

"That makes a lot of sense," I agreed. "Albert is quite the visionary. Whenever I gaze at his masterpieces, I am always intrigued with these particular places and people by wanting to visit these distant destinations."

"That is my brother's sole goal: unite the planet. Hopefully, we will never have to immerse ourselves in another world war," Pierre avowed in bated breath.

Pierre notified me that Jacques is not doing well; he is mentally suffering from the war. He has memory lapses, fits of rage, and inaudible dialogue. He lost his home, and he is now living with his older sister and her family. Sadly, he has to be locked in their basement to prevent him from hurting himself and others. Also, they have to hide and to lock any sharp objects from him. Pierre and I conversed for over an hour, and we realized how blessed we are. Our lives are definitely not perfect, but we survived a ruthless and vicious war with our minds and bodies intact. Most importantly, we are still alive. So many of our battlefield comrades suffered shrapnel wounds to the face which almost permanently disfigured them. Pierre reported that a new medical technology, plastic or reconstructive surgery is performed at London's Queen's hospital to give dignity back to our soldiers by artfully removing their grotesque scars of war and attempting to make them look as normal as they did before they were injured.

Heather finally gets off our couch to clean herself. Once she is dressed, she demurely asks if she did anything to embarrass herself or make me upset. To her amazement, I say that she was quite amorous and well-behaved. She gives me a huge hug. I show her the photographs that Pierre sent me. She adores them and gapes at them over and over due to the multiple hues. I tell her that Pierre's brother is a very wealthy philanthropist changing the world with one photo at a time. Hours pass as I explained the many locations of each picture to Heather. We finally retire to bed together. We still visited speakeasies, but it is a very dangerous venture. Because there is no segregation, I often receive dirty looks from white men when I am with Heather because they perceive Heather as a white woman. The District of Columbia is still below the Mason Dixie Line, so Southern traditions reign. Heather and I decide to try a different establishment: The Tabard Inn, which happens to be entirely owned and operated by women. We have to love the roaring twenties because women are active and productive citizens.

The Tabard Inn is overwhelmingly White. Heather and I did not see any other blacks or people of color inside this saloon, for that matter. It was exceedingly upper echelon, but the clientele stared at us as to convey, "What are you (me in particular) Nigga doing here?" Our experience is chafing because no one waited on us. Heather became very athirst and asks where is the waiter to take our orders for patrons. The only response that she receives is from a drunkard White woman. "Why did you bring that Nigga in here? Your own kind aren't good enough for you!?" she scoffed.

"You dumb, cracker bitch, I am a Nigga too!" Heather yells.

Heather is stone-sober; she didn't have a single drink in her. I love to see her fiery nature emerge like a volcano when she is not drunk. Heather removes her shoes and throws her hands up to make fists. As quick as lightening,

Heather smacks the shit out of that white bitch's face because of her uncontrollable umbrage. Then she rips the majority of her hair from her scalp, making the white marble floor look like a patch of burnt sienna animal fur resting on it. This is a classic bar brawl because spectators take sides; it lasted for about an hour. This bout is just as exciting as the boxing match between Jack Johnson and Jack Dempsey. Heather replicates Johnson's defensive moves by dodging her sloppy opponent's counterpunches. When the opportunity presents itself, Heather jabs the woman so hard in her torso that she renders her unconscious. Half of the crowd roars for Heather as we flee the scene. Of course, no one could call the police for help because this barrage of blows happens inside an illegal establishment. After it was said and done, the female version of Dempsey has a black eye and a bruised left cheekbone, while Heather victorious in this fracas is free of any mars on her exquisite body. However, her natty clothes are demolished. Her rolled stockings have multiple runs, her dress is torn from the front and rear, and her favorite hat is ripped on the edges. Her shoes are still intact because I held them for her. I never knew that Heather has such a mighty right uppercut. We really have a solid bond between one another, and times are really good for us. I never imagined that our relationship would evolve to this degree. I love Heather, but I'm not in love with her like I am with Barrington. I consider her as a great companion.

Heather and I developed a new hobby: going to see motion pictures. Heather loved to be scared, so we saw, 'Nosferatu'. The Knickerbocker theater has the best films. We try to attend weekly since prohibition is still the law of the land and we didn't have to fight our way inside the movie shows. The winter of 1922 is much worse than the one in 1899 because Washington, DC is completely paralyzed by another brutal blizzard. Heather is clean and sober because I contend that she really enjoys going to the movies together with me. Again, Heather has traded one addiction for another: looking at picture shows. We want to escape the boredom of being snowed in, so we are going to watch another moving picture. On January 28th, we elect to see the film, 'Get-Rich-Quick Wallingford'. It was snowing heavily two days prior to when we are supposed to attend. Our dates, to the picture shows, are synonymous to when we courted during our teens. For the first time in my life, I question my sexuality. I wondered if I was really gay or not. In the early morning, the sky was still dark and gray. Doom and gloom consume me, yet it has nothing to do with the inclement weather. It continues to snow and the silent film does not begin until 7 p.m.; therefore, I really was not that concerned. However, my gut has a disturbing sensation, like a warning from our creator. I dreamt about Holly the previous night, but I could not remember what the dream entailed. However, I do know that it was something foreboding and troubling. We are both dressed to the nines. We decided that it was better to walk instead of driving because the snow is steadily falling. Ironically, it is not that cold, so we didn't have to worry about slipping on any ice. The walk from our residence to the theater is barely 30 minutes. I watch Heather's face, as I purchase the tickets. She gushes with total enthusiasm. She closes her beautiful multicolor parasol as we enter the picture show. We hold hands as we sit next to one another, anxiously awaiting to see this highly acclaimed film. Heather wore white lace gloves for a fashion statement instead of warmth. Heather wears the best accoutrements; they are always ultra-elegant. As soon as the picture show begins, Heather and I could not stop laughing. It is so hilarious. Moreover, the heartiness of laughter would fill the entire theater at times. Occasional eruptions of cachinnation sounded from the audience, which comprised of hundreds of spectators. The live orchestra is phenomenal, as well. Between the outbursts of chortle, I have an urge to let Heather know that I genuinely love her.

"I love you Heather," I announce proudly. She bends over close to me and kisses me on the cheek.

"I luvs you too, Peanut," she whispers lovingly.

Our attention reconveys to the funny film. Two hours into the show, boisterous laughter perdures. I apprise Heather that I have to use the restroom, so I walk as briskly as I could to ensure that I would not miss too much of the moving picture show. As soon as I enter the lobby, another blustering noise accompanies the hearty peal of laughter, yet it resonates with war bombs. The entire roof collapses; I could not locate Heather anywhere. The roof and balcony crashed to the floor with such ferocity and speed that the doors and windows blew open from the compressed air inside the auditorium. The freezing gust of wind piercing through the ceiling jolts me towards the exit. Patrons are screaming and running for cover trying to locate the exit. When the dust clears, I could see dead bodies covered with concrete, plaster and bricks. My heart stops. Heather is pinned to the wall by twisted steel beams with half of her torso missing crushed by the fallen balcony with a big grin on her face. Her eyes are wide open and as pretty as they are, they are now rendered lifeless. I do not know where her legs are located, but I carried what is left of Heather outside. The entire scene replicates a battlefield during the war, where the bodies of disfigured dead men, women, and children are spewed throughout the facility. Heather's demise optically replicates the crucifixion of Jesus Christ. Even members of the orchestra died while forcefully playing alongside the picture show. I am so in shock that I didn't notice that the ambulance and police had arrived. It literally looks like mortar bombs imploded inside the Knickerbocker. I frantically hold Heather as tight as I could, but paramedics pry her severed and bloody body from me to put her inside a body bag. Paramedics assume that I am injured because my entire torso is blanketed with Heather's blood. I try to contain her entrails by wrapping them with my arms while holding her in an upward position. I just can't wrap my head around regarding what happened due to the surrealism of it all. Heather and I just wanted to laugh, bond, and have a good time by intimately enjoying each other's company. I embed so much guilt because if I never went to the bathroom, I would probably be dead too. My brief absence saved my life. After a thorough investigation, we learn that the weight of the snow caused the entire roof to falter. With this particular death, I could not come to terms with forgiving myself. I am gravely incensed because the newspapers compare this disaster with the war. I am a World War I veteran. Thus, the analogies among the Spanish Influenza, and the Knickerbocker theater with World War I are cruel and insensitive. These reporters should try fighting in an actual war before comparing global tragedies with international skirmishes. At 33, my entire family is decimated. To add insult to injury, the autopsy from the coroner's report concludes that Heather was four months pregnant. The gender is undetermined because the lower half of the fetus was also sundered due to the fact the child would have been a breech birth. Nevertheless, I survived both World War I without a scratch and the Knickerbocker Snowstorm calamity.

I deduce that Holly was trying to prognosticate about this predicament during Barrington's séances and in my dream that I had the previous evening before the picture show. Holly donned such a forlorn expression, which is so unusual in comparison to her normally upbeat demeanor. A total of 98 people perished from the roof collapse. Even a popular politician, Andrew Jackson Barchfeld, met the same fate as Heather. Speaking of the war, Barchfeld's parents are German immigrants from Prussia; he was a Republican from the U.S. House of Representatives who was born in Pittsburg, Pennsylvania. Heather's death is such a brutal blow because of its unpredictability. She has to have a closed-casket funeral because her body is literally cut in half at her torso. She is the only child, and we did not produce any living offspring together. Heather's parents are devastated by their loss, but they told me that I will always be like a son to them. I let the Widgeon family and Pierre know about Heather's demise only after the funeral. They both invited me to stay with them or the other option that is they would visit me, but I declined both invitations. I just want to be alone. I slept a lot and ate rarely. Days would go on end and I would not get out of bed. Alma tries to persuade me to get fresh air and eat. My melancholy tarried along with me for months. I thought to myself that losing Heather hurts immensely because I actually deeply cared for her. Not too long ago, I would not have concerned myself about her passing. Life is so capricious. I am inconsolable. I always thought that she would die from alcohol poisoning, abduction or a bar brawl. May is finally here and the Lincoln Memorial is almost complete. I visited this beautiful edifice and had my photograph taken in front of it which I will cherish for years. The reflecting pool and interior lighting still have to be finished. The most spectacular effect is more than 1,800 cherry blossom trees are blooming and mirroring themselves within the reflecting pool by taking narcissistic stances. Their intense rose-colored flowers sing with joy and pride among one another. I am disappointed because these ethereal images are only displayed in black and white. Hence, I am spoiled by Albert Khan's magnanimous polychrome photographs.

I found a hobby to help me combat my depression by frequently visiting the Krazy Kat Klub. Open homosexuality is so widespread and accepted here, that I cannot resist. I rarely drank anything; instead, I just had intense sex with the male customers who frequented this illegal establishment. I had intercourse with men individually and participated in threesomes. I didn't even know their names. I give and receive fellatio; I initiate and accept sodomy. I did not discriminate because I had sex with white men, drunk and sober. It makes no difference to me. My intention is to have as much illicit one-night stands in order to fuck the pain away without enveloping any emotional attachments. One evening, I had sex with five different men. My penis was so sore as an aftermath of various sexual positions. My erections would last for at least 30 minutes. I had to take cold showers just to get my penis to deflate. When I had my fill of lustful lasciviousness, I went home and slept it off, simply to do it again another day. Sadly, my slumber offers no solace because I would often have wet dreams where my underwear harbors a chock-full of sperm.

Unbeknownst to me, my former student: Hank from Howard University watched me have sex with multiple partners in the men's restroom. I am so single-minded on relieving my sufferings that I am inattentive to my surroundings. In addition, I no longer have Heather to conceal my homosexual activities. I went to the Howard University Library to grade some papers, and Hank rudely interrupted me.

"Professor Williams, do you remember me?" Hank asked slyly.

"Of course, I do. How are you?" I replied.

"I am swell. You don't strike me as a person who would visit a speakeasy," Hank insinuated.

"I beg your pardon," I angrily stated.

"I saw you at the Krazy Kat one evening," Hank stipulated.

"I guess we are both complicit," I smirked.

"Perhaps for being inside of a speakeasy. Yet, you were involved in other extracurricular activities, Professor Williams," he baited.

"Why don't you say what you mean and mean what you say, Hank?" I insisted. Hank's aura is sheathed with profound perfidy.

"I did not know that you are gay," Hank said.

I never replied to his accusation. I just listened to him. He revealed that he observed my homosexual acts and became sexually stimulated watching me fuck other men. I thought to myself that he is nothing more than a bombastic psychopath.

"Are you gay, Hank?" I inquired.

"No, not at all. I just get incredibly stimulated watching men have sex with other men, Professor Williams," Hank confessed. "I masturbate profusely whenever I think about men being sexually intertwined."

"I hope that we can keep this information private between the two of us, Hank," I implored.

"Absolutely, Professor Williams. Keeping secrets is my specialty," Hank declared.

After learning about Hank's discovery, I stopped going to the Krazy Kat. Something about Hank is exceedingly untrustworthy. Holly continues to visit me from the other side. She apprises me that my life will only get better after enduring so many losses. She let me know that Heather is happy and at peace with herself. As beautiful as she physically was in this life, she constantly struggled with having any self-worth. Her dilemma was that she always compared herself to others. Because she passed for white as a Negro, she perceived herself as inferior to the Caucasian race by simply being labeled as a Colored. I am grateful that Holly informed me of Heather's spiritual evolution; however, I had to interject Hank's interactions with me to Holly. She confirms that my suspicions are on point. Thankfully, Hank has no tangible evidence, like photographs of me inside the Krazy Kat or witnesses that could vouch for him. Holly explicitly emphasizes that I should keep it this way. Holly specifies that Hank is homosexual and plans to blackmail me. Holly also stresses that Hank detests his gay nature. As soon as she appears, she is gone in an instant. I forgot Alma is still working in our residence. She knocks on my door and asks if I am alright because she hears voices. I assure her that I am fine. She let me know that Barrington had called and he wanted me to urgently return his telephone call.

Summer is almost here. I prefer to entertain myself at home by listening to the radio because it brings back wonderful childhood memories for me. They play the song: 'Harlem Choc'late Babies on Parade' by James P. Johnson frequently. I adore hearing his masterful piano playing. Sometimes, I am so bewitched with the music that I lose track of time. Something rather strange and exciting happened on June 14, 1922, when President Warren G. Harding makes an announcement regarding a dedication to a memorial site for the composer, Francis Scott Key. No one has ever heard a U.S. president speak on the radio prior to this day. This is really an uplifting and pleasant surprise. Wow, the president of the United States of America talks on the radio, really? This is absolutely amazing. Being that this is my new hobby, this medium simulates that the president of the United States of America is conversing directly with me and other commoners. I can't emphasize how technology is exponentially growing throughout my 32 years on Earth. It's awesomely amazing.

Chapter 4
"Periódico de Ayer"
by Hector Lavoe

The Garvey movement achieves international success and the Widgeons offer me a formal assignation to attend Garvey's speech, entitled, "The Principals of the Universal Negro Improvement Association." It is Thanksgiving, and Howard University is on vacation until the following semester. I willingly pack my bags and take the train to Harlem to witness this monumental event on the principles of the UNIA. I brought my favorite souvenir from Paris during my service in the war, which is a 35 mm Le Cent Vue Model One camera. Garvey's speech is mesmerizing, and it instills the same degree of pride within me when I first witnessed native Nubian Egyptians living in Aswan via Albert Khan's polychrome photographs. My Negro ancestors built the mighty pyramids and created civilization long before any European could conceive of these vast triumphs. This genre of knowledge can never be taken away from anyone, be it society or systematic regime. I understood the root causes of white supremacy when Napoleon Bonaparte blew off the nose of the great Sphinx because it was Negroid and represented the African diaspora. This vicious act was a castigation on Negritude! Most people don't realize that Egypt is a nation located in Africa. Native Egyptians labelled their nation Kemet, which means Black Land. Harlem is such a mecca of Negro National opulence because one can find and see famous black writers, entrepreneurs, doctors, lawyers, educators and entertainers. Amazingly, I caught a glimpse of the glamourous and gorgeous civil rights activist, Josephine Baker, in the metro station. I quickly rushed over to her to ask if I could take a photograph with her. Baker did not hesitate and told a member of her entourage to photograph us together. I proudly display this picture in my office at Howard University and sent a copy to Pierre in France. This is such a marvelous finale to my trip to Harlem.

I wonder how Otis and other enslaved Negroes during slavery on various plantations would be empowered and transformed if they knew about Queen Tiye of the 18th dynasty of Egypt and her relationship to King Tutankhamun. Hence, Queen Tiye is King Tut's grandmother. Another powerful Egyptian image that would have credentialed Negro slaves is King Piye of the 25th dynasty, who has a very dark complexion with Negroid features. As a young boy, I would have more dignity and love for my race and the entire African diaspora if I learned about these Egyptian icons. Arab colonization is just as caustic as European colonialism because Arabs conquered the African continent, enslaving, murdering and torturing African people on their own land. This is the reason why Islam, date trees, and denigration flourishes on the African Continent. As a university professor, I appreciate Garvey's emphasis on empowering African people and teaching them authentic history to boost their self-esteem, White washing history is not only dangerous, but digressive for the African Diaspora and other people of color who have experienced White Supremacist domination. Negroes need to own our children's curriculum instruction and control pedagogical materials taught at the collegiate level, as well, to ensure positive and proactive Black societies throughout the diaspora and win the fight of this contemporary cultural war.

Garvey's tenet on separation from European societies in order to preserve our dignity and Negritude saliently predominates his discourse. He officially condemns Negroes assimilating into White culture because Europeans will never equate themselves to us. Alternatively, White assimilation leads to the cultural denigration and demise of melanated people worldwide. It is always a delight to be with the Widgeon family. However, my time is limited because I had to assess finals for my students at Howard University. I wanted to stay longer and perhaps reconnect with Barrington, but time does not allow. I plan to present the major themes enveloped in his speech and Garvey's movement to my dean in order to include this information in my curriculum. Comparably, Howard University is a prime example of an educational institution premised upon Pan-Africanism, as it is dedicated solely for people of the African diaspora. Regrettably, 1922 proves to be a tough year for Garvey because he divorces his first wife, Amy Ashwood, who is an eminent feminist. Additionally, his newspaper: 'The Negro World' ceases circulation in Africa and is confiscated due to financial difficulties. The worst event of this difficult year is Garvey's incarceration and the dissolution of his Black Star organization. Barrington and I believe that any entity that challenges white supremacy will face severe consequences. Garvey's businesses are unjustly disrupted, and he is arrested on baseless charges. Haiti is another example of a global White backlash for being victorious over the British, French and Spanish troops, which led to it being the first Negro republic in the Western Hemisphere to be free from European slavery and oppression. Just last year, the innocent and successful Negros of Tulsa, Oklahoma, endured a hideous and lethal assault by European Americans for simply being affluent, proud, and progressive without the help or intermingling of whites. Intrusive Caucasians minded the business affairs of these particular Negroes and deemed that they are achieving too much wealth and progress, even though they lived separately and apart from whites. These innocent Negroes are attacked via air raids and the aftermath replicates numerous battlefields in France during World War I. Hence, I deem that the Tulsa Massacre should be compared to a global war. This bloodbath happened because the Coloreds of Tulsa exude black Excellence, and whites resented it.

Pierre is ecstatic to receive the photograph of Josephine Baker and I together; Baker is practically an icon in France. The virulence of antisemitism and the public prominence of anti-Semites permeate most of Europe. Moreover, the Russian Empire and Romania are particularly problematic. Certain socio-cultural milieus: such as political parties and publishers in France and Germany, are emulating this cruel bigotry towards Jewry communities. Pierre is Jewish and very afraid because Europeans have a history of horrific abuses toward its Jewish diaspora since the Middle Ages. Pierre always reminds me that our ethnicities share this cruel commonality. He also warns that homosexuals and Gypsies are in peril by the dominant Anglo-Saxon, Slavic, and Aryan subgroups obsessed and controlled by fascism. I wonder why Nazis abhor homosexuals, so I asked Pierre. Pierre explains that it goes back to Eugenics in the United States. Gays cannot genetically reproduce. Thus, white gays are stunting the proliferation of their respective races. Pierre sent me some racist caricatures depicting Jews in local and national newspapers throughout France. I try to reassure Pierre that this racial hatred is probably a phase and will pass, so he should not worry or give it too much thought. I told Pierre that he could visit and stay with me indefinitely should a tangible threat manifest itself. Fortunately, his eldest brother, Albert, is a world traveler, visiting exotic places like Japan for his 'Archives of the Planet' project. Albert is exceedingly generous and shares his wealth with his siblings, so money is never a problem for Pierre. Albert's acquired wealth as a banker skyrocketed due to his philanthropy. Albert offers scholarships to interns learning about photography, promotes female employees, and pays for his clients' international travels. As a university professor, I deem negative propaganda is an extremely dangerous strategy to encourage the masses to dehumanize and ostracize a certain group of people. For the past 400 years in the United States, or 1619, Native American and African atrocities are so commonplace by propaganda and laws that desensitization permeates the majority of the masses. These oppressive practices begin to normalize the oppression of melanated people and even create melanated accomplices who unconsciously aid with the tenets of white supremacist ideology on a global scale. In essence, racial oppression is ubiquitous in the United States of America and the entire world.

My dean approves my idea to incorporate Garvey's assertion on separatism of the races and his controversial accordance with the Ku Klux Klan. I anxiously anticipate designing my syllabus for the following semester. Now that I look back, Barrington has really made a significant influence on my life in a myriad of ways. I am always conflicted regarding my sexuality. To make matters worse, furtively concealing my sexual orientation is burdensome. I am not free to be who I am. This incessant façade of my public persona is burgeoning my private lifestyle. I did not indulge with any fraternities during my collegiate matriculation; however, I decided to partake in one fraternity, as a working professional. I pledged Kappa Alpha Psi because this particular organization was the target of KKK torment and harassment at Indiana University. The core always seems to be stemmed from the same reason: Negritude coupled with preeminence disturbs the consciousness of many of our White counterparts. It is laughable of how narcissistic some Caucasians are by their intimidation of black excellence and how they feel the need to quell it by any means necessary. The Kappa fraternity is committed to community service by helping our brothers and sisters who are impoverished and necessitate food and clothing. My fraternity also offers scholarships to aid young Black men with their collegiate education. I am quite proud of the altruism that my fraternity instills within me. I sport my crimson and cream colors, representing Kappa Alpha

Psi whenever and wherever I can. Moreover, it is a segue for future job and social opportunities worldwide, not to mention the close comradery that we share with other men. For the next few years, I immersed myself into my work. I published an article for the Howard Review on the importance of black separatism and how this precept empowers the African diaspora. I was promoted to assistant dean of students in the philosophy department. My work is my new obsession to ameliorate my loneliness. I have no pets to comfort me, so I am appreciative that Alma is still alive and well.

Violent crime continues to escalate because of Prohibition. Drive-by shootings using automatic weapons like the Thompson submachine gun permeate major cities, especially Chicago and New York. The Fourth Estate reports daily on the mob gangs killing innocent people and other gangsters involved with bootlegging. I share the opinion with many that prohibition needs to end because mass murders are too frequent and macabre. The newspapers have no shame with revealing multiple photographs of graphic gunshot wounds, barbaric beatings, and dead bodies. Loss of life percolates within the United States. The U.S. public is becoming numb because this bloodshed is so normalized. It is not only dangerous living in this country, but it is also dismal. I am ready to vacate this place. Organized crime continues to outsmart the law by devising new devices and evolving new schemes to import illegal liquor into the United States. The dichotomy associated with Prohibition is cuttingly sharp. Mobsters amass awe-inspiring wealth, whilst committing the most brutal crimes imaginable. Fallen casualties of bootlegging wars overshadow the roaring twenties.

I frequently visit Barrington in Harlem, where we take leisurely walks through Mount Morris Park in the dark. Here, we steal kisses from one another while admiring the sparce, but glorious cherry blossom trees meticulously demarcating tamed geographic trekking paths. Barrington sold his rowhouse in Georgetown and his father's business. He is making a hefty salary in Harlem from bootlegging liquor. Barrington was not directly involved with the sales of illegal spirits, but he would alert bootleggers of any police presence possibly obstructing any transactions of illicit intoxicants. He does all of this in retaliation to Hoover's destruction of Garvey's enterprise. Marcus started to rebel against his father, and Barrington has no clue as to why his only son is behaving with such insurgency. Little did we know that Marcus inadvertently walked in on us having sex on Barrington's kitchen floor when I sodomized Barrington. Marcus perceived my sodomy with his father as pure evil like a snake slithering on his father's back. I vividly remember this particular sex act because Barrington and I were so horny that night that we could not wait and wanted to have intercourse with one another hastily. Byron shares this secret with Barrington, who in turn tells me the reason for Marcus' unpleasant reactions towards him. Strangely, whenever I encounter Marcus, he receives me with a pleasant respect. I found this to be rather odd. I bid my farewells to the Widgeon family before I take my tour back to France. Alma is becoming frail. Afterall, she is 68 years-old. She has a strong constitution. She never married or had children, but she always exudes self-contentment and equanimity. Pierre invited me to France to spend time with him. Pierre is also single and has no children, but he is not homosexual. Pierre bought a first-class ticket for me on the ocean liner: *SS Île de France*. I plan to go during my annual sabbatical in 1927.

I stayed with the Widgeons on my way to France because my ship departed from the port of New York City. I studied the city intricately. I discovered that New York is literally a maritime city because it has approximately 520 miles of coastline, more than Los Angeles, San Francisco, Miami, and Boston combined. Yes, it has the Hudson River, but New York City is more oceanic. For Marcus' sake, Barrington and I agreed to never be physical again. We never have sex, kiss or cuddle. Without a doubt, I still have sexual urges for Barrington on a daily basis; however, I can't fathom the depth of trauma that we imposed upon Marcus. Can you imagine any child unexpectedly encountering his or her parent having homosexual sex when the child is totally unaware of this particular parent's sexual orientation? Not to mention, that the parent is legally married to a heterosexual spouse. I hope that one day Marcus will be able to forgive his father and understand why he kept this secret from him. We are still intimate because of the personal information that we always exchange between us, but our intimacy only extends verbally. I took a vow of celibacy. I don't know how long this phase of my life will last, but I believe that it is something that I need to do. Holly did not come around as much. Her visits started to fade. I questioned Barrington about this aspect of transitioning. He explained that our deceased will begin a journey to another paradigm, which is usually reincarnation. When this occurs, it is difficult for the soul to reenact their former lives. Alma has to care for my parents' rowhouse for an entire year. To subdue the eerie loneliness, I decide to rent out three rooms on the second floor inside my parents' rowhouse only to Howard University female students. After my confrontation with Hank, I do not want any temptations or loose ends inside my home and sanctity. My bedroom is located on the third floor. In my absence, Alma would house-sit and sleep in my bedroom.

I brought my finest clothes and some books to read on the long journey over the open seas. The ship is styled with Art Deco, that stimulates and energizes your senses. This ship oozes with opulence and epitomizes luxury. The gaudy chandeliers, the sumptuous dual wood-laden stairways, colorful and bright wallpaper, and exquisite cuisine make this weeklong voyage like a royal paradise fit for kings and queens. It has an amazing bar extending three decks, so thirsty Americans at sea can get their fill of alcohol because Prohibition is still the law of the land. Gigantic champagne fountains roar offering bubbly blissfulness. I did not miss any of the amenities aground because she had a barbershop, movie theater, indoor swimming pool, and an infirmary. I refuse to enter picture shows because of how Heather died. The trauma associated with this place has put tremendous trepidation in my soul. Now that I think about it, I have not been inside a picture show since Heather's passing. I can't get the grisly image of Heather's severed body pinned to the wall —open eyes and scarlet blood that matched her lipstick and fingernail polish—out of my head. Heather would have loved this floating palace. The elegance, food service, sleeping amenities, and art décor are absolutely awesome. The sea bass, ribs, beef sirloin with horseradish, and the desserts are phenomenal. They remind me of holiday dining growing up in Georgetown. Pierre is a great friend because he spent $1,800.00 for my ticket. I want to repay him, but Pierre is the type of individual not to accept anything in return because his heart is pure. The trip is so relaxing; I have not been this calm for a long time. I sat on the deck and got a dark suntan. I napped for a few hours in the lounge chair while the sun's beams showered my body and I heard faint background sounds of laughter, swishing water, and chattery colloquy. The only drawback with this international trip is that some whites would either stare at me to see if I was someone famous or look through me, as if I was totally invisible. The heat is sweltering during the summers and this also includes sailing on the ship. Giant ice cubes are chipped with an ice pick by the ship's crew. Yes, holy, yes —ice picks, electric fans, and summertime go hand and hand. Inside, I would sit by the fan with melting ice transmuting into water while dripping through my fingers and flowing down the back of my neck. I am so accustomed to being wet and sticky during the summer months because this is the only known method of lowering our body temperatures. At home, I would simply grab ice from the icebox and chip the block with an ice pick. Then, I would put it inside a towel to temper the intoxicating effects of humidity in the District of Columbia. I can definitely think of another activity that soaks my clothes, and that is having anal sex whilst being dressed. Anyway, let's just stick to the weather.

I didn't realize how much I miss France. Being in France enables me to fully actualize what an authentic human being is. I blend in with everyone around me without conspicuously being harassed for simply belonging to the Negro race. Strolling along The Avenue des Champs-Élysées, the aromas bring back pleasant and painful memories simultaneously. The smell of baked bread, the wet fur of dogs dining in cafes, the sweet air after it rains, replicating honey and coffee, as I long for Claudette. Even the clothes shops emit scents of roses, lavender, cigar smoke, and black peppercorns, slowly seeping outside of their doors and open windows. My mind is completely transformed to a state of bliss. The unbearable sorrow of missing my entire family and Barrington transmuted into euphoria. It has been a decade since I was here and their fashion sense remains stupendous. The French really know how to dress impeccably, with the utmost style and elegance in the subtlest ways. Pierre moved from Alsace to Paris. He resides in a beautiful five-bedroom apartment with two floors. His place replicates a miniature version of the Palace of Versailles. We visit Versailles, but it is so overwhelmingly large that we are unable to see all of the stunningly beautiful artwork on one tarry. Pierre tries to hide his ostentatious wealth. From the outside, his residence appears small. But, once you're inside, it is humongous. He has wall-to-wall, floor-to-ceiling overlay of his brother's stunningly-colored photographs from around the world. Pierre's walls are a visual mirage endlessly enticing our eyes. As ravishing as Pierre's apartment is, diametrically, his outdoor surroundings are antipodally hideous due to grotesque graffiti of Jewish people depicted with exaggerated noses being compared to rats and other vermin. A plethora of posters posted outside businesses throughout Paris spewing, "Jews will not replace us!" This phrase exemplifies the profound paranoia towards Jewry, envisioning a ludicrous and delusional 'replacement theory' ideology where other races will annihilate the Anglo-Saxons and Aryans simply due to genome dominance. I do remember some French when I was here during the war. The defamation of Jewish synagogues in France is scary. Coupled with the gross misuse of the Star of David written in a perverse and cruel alphabetic symbology in crimson paint. The most despicable of locales are elementary schools forced to exhibit these racist illustrations. No one encountered any physical abuse, but the threatening writings on exterior walls are signs of the evil that is to come. Such horrific statements are the following: 'Death to Jews!' I vividly recall when my mother taught Holly and I this maxim: "Sticks and stones may break my bones, but words can never hurt me." As common as this phrase may be, it is untrue because some of my most painful moments were caused by a person's verbiage. Alarmingly, this environment mirrors the Negros' living experience in white-controlled America. Fascism is alive and well in France.

"Pierre, I am so devastated to see such blatant hatred being spewed towards the international Jewry community," I said.

"Peanut, please allow me to share a sacred Kabbalistic quotation from the Torah for handling life's most difficult situations," Pierre insisted. "The worst manifestation of egoism is arrogance and conceit, from the Talmud, Sota."

"Always remember that our egos keep us apart from divinity. Gradually, these antisemitic messages are seeping into politics and propaganda. Adopted from the United States, Eugenics is a great motivating factor to implement hatred and ostracism of the Jewish race throughout Europe. An elite group of people (wealthy Anglo-Saxons and Aryans) decide who procreates based on sound physical and mental health. If a person is deemed unhealthy or not physically aesthetic, he or she will be punished through sterilization via tubal litigation for women and vasectomy for men. Hence, their birthrights are strictly prohibited, as well as their body functions. During the Spanish and Portuguese inquisitions, Jews were ousted from Europe and sent to the Americas. Decimation begins subtly, then a crescendo erupts into a barbaric, irrational removal of our race, whether it is a forced move to a new physical location or attempted genocide," Pierre proclaims.

Albert's photographs are exceptional because they literally take you to the places that he visits due to the prisms of color enveloped in his film. Thus, we are literally inside each miniature canvass. I really want to meet him, but he was on an expedition with his photography team in Canada for the next two months. Albert's vivid creations keep our minds occupied from this blistering, burgeoning movement throughout Europe. Pierre hung my photograph with Josephine Baker in a beautifully copper frame in his sitting room. Unexpectedly, I resonate most with his beautifully framed photograph of the goldish-orange corn poppy because it is a metaphor for veterans of World War I. Most of our fighting obstructed the growth and potential blooms of the corn poppy. Yet, this flower's endurance thrives in spite of the horrors of war on its sacred and holy fertile ground, thus, connecting it eternally to the first global war. Paris has such high cultural capital. We visited the Louvre Museum, dined on frog legs, drank the finest local wine, and ate escargot. The pairing of the variety of cheeses, bread, and wines is so phenomenal that it makes a meal on its own accord. Pierre pleasantly surprised me with a homemade, quintessential Jewish dessert called, Charlotte Russe.

"I hear that this treat is quite popular in Brooklyn, New York," Pierre says.

"I've never ventured into Brooklyn because I always roam Harlem. I will definitely make a point to buy some on my next trip to New York City. These are delectable. The cream makes them so light and not too sweet, but very satisfying at the same time. You can't just eat one," I declared.

Walking along the grassy, verdant Champ de Mars gazing at the Eiffel Tower, I pensively thought how Paris is designed like the U.S. capital. Paris' iconic river, the Seine, winds around the city the same way the Potomac twists around the District of Colombia. But its cultural sense aligns more with Harlem. Paris honors Negro cosmopolitanism. Jazz is played everywhere, and black stars perform here frequently. Like World War I black soldiers, Negros acquire a redemption that is lost in America. Exhilaration fills my body from head to toe because on Halloween we are going to see Paul Robeson give a recital of Negro spirituals at the Salle Gaveau. My favorite rendition from him is 'Swing Low, Sweet Chariot'. In spite of limited advertising, all 1,500 seats are occupied, and about 500 people had to be turned away from the doors from lack of seating. At the end of the show, Mr. Robeson receives a standing ovation which is so highly deserved. These venues make me so proud to be part of the African diaspora. The first people who came to my mind are Meredith and Barrington. Meredith loves to sing spirituals because of her in-depth background with the Fisk Jubilee singers, and they both admire Robeson's consciousness regarding Black empowerment and intellectualism. I called them and apprised them of our wonderful experience at the concert the next day. The Widgeons are delighted, but they only want to visit the African continent. I told them that Pierre is Jewish, and his people experience similar discriminations, as Negros do in the United States. I briefly saw Antoinette. I treated her to dinner at a small café. She is still grieving Claudette's death. I offered to perform a séance, so she could see her again, but she politely declined. Antoinette is consumed with the blues, and there is nothing that I can do to motivate her spirit to embrace peace. I let her know that I am here for her in any way that she needs, but I could tell that she preferred to be alone (tout seul).

I am celibate solely because of Marcus. I never want to be responsible for any person's trauma, especially children. Pierre and I retire to bed. I have the second floor to myself and like a ton of bricks, I start bawling in the bed. I didn't realize that I am still mourning my cats', parents', Holly's and Heather's deaths. My repressed Gehenna has been illusive to me until it rose from my core like flowing lava does from a volcano. I compensated my grief by having promiscuous sex or burying my emotions under my work. It has been years, but their capricious departures seem like yesterday. Now that I am still, I am finally able to really intuit my sorrow regarding my familial losses. It's funny how trauma stealthily sneaks and creeps upon us. I can't stop crying and my eyes are totally bloodshot. My chest hurts from my sonorous sobbing. I weep for days because I have an overwhelming loom of loneliness encapsulating me. I take advantage of the rainstorm and promenade along the Pont Neuf Bridge, where the rain disguises my teardrops like a chameleon's camouflage, hiding it in plain sight. My tears become one with the Seine River. Pierre is so empathetic and compassionate because he fully understands my dark melancholy. He gave me a big hug, and I laid my head on his shoulders, like I used to do with my mother. This catharsis cleansed my soul. As I peer out of the window, observing the gorgeous pink gentle giants, the receptivity of cherry blossoms hems my blues.

Holly no longer visits me. Perhaps her absence is augmenting my intense lamentation. It is almost freeing to have an innocent platonic relationship with a man, no strings or attachments. Pierre is like a brother that I never had. I let him borrow Barrington's book: 'The Rising Tide of Color: The Threat Against White World-Supremacy' by Lothrop Stoddard. I explained to Pierre that Jews are perceived as Semitics, like their Arab cousins. Thus, members of the White race fear their genetic annihilation by Semitic ethnicities and people of color. I certainly hope that the defamation of Jews is just a shallow phase in Europe and it will not lead to the cruel brutality that Coloreds experience in the United States for centuries.

"You are simply a novelty in France. There are not too many of us living there; thus, you are not a threat. Don't be delusional because wherever Whites dominate, they will always try to subjugate non-whites. They are the most tribal beings on planet Earth," Barrington staunchly asserts.

"With all of my education, wealth, and light skin, I incessantly experience dehumanization while living in the US. Yet, France allows me to feel human, equality, freedom and pride," I fervently disagree with him.

"Living in Liberia or any other nation on the African continent will give us our desired humanity, dignity, and authentic sovereignty," Barrington pontificated.

I didn't want Barrington to mar my perfect vacation, so I told him that I will call him later and thanked him for his insightful opinions. My doldrum moods endured Paris' winter, but Spring birthed a surprisingly inner joy within me. Like my beloved hometown, Paris is draped and adorned with Cherry Blossom trees. One of my favorite stomping grounds is Montmartre, which houses the majestic Sacre Coeur Basilica. It is lined with artists, lovers and people-watchers. Time flies by when I indulge in this activity —watching strangers and simultaneously fantasizing about their respective lives. The scenery is so tranquil that I sit for hours simply observing my surroundings. Alongside the cheerful chatter, I can hear crickets chirping in the distance. The weather is perfect, with the sun shining and a light and brisk breeze flowing through me. Cherry blossoms also inundate the Champs de Mars, but the energy there is so busy because tourists can't wait to see the iconic Eiffel Tower. Tears begin to well in my eyes as I admired the surreal beauty of the cherry blossom trees. Alternatively, these tears are of immense joy. It seems that my life has come full circle —a literal 360-

degree trajectory. I made an unofficial rite of spiritual passage by witnessing these dazzling rose-colored living beings. Almost 4,000 miles sequester these cherry blossom trees from the ones blossoming in my hometown, where my life is rooted. The unfolding of my life reveals that I am never alone, by any means, because creation always thrives around us. We just need to take the time to smell and behold the flowers.

Chapter 5
"Yamuna Tira Vihari"
by Alice Coltrane

Finding myself in Paris, France is an invaluable moxie. This year exposed me to confront deep-rooted truths and how to handle crises in a proactive way. Paying my respects to Claudette's grave is also a gut-wrenching occasion, especially because I missed her funeral. Her tombstone has both his birthname and her gender-altered one. This feat is quite triumphant for what she stood for during her life. Spirits of the dead no longer converse with me. I want to do another séance, but it would be without the Widgeons. I am not confident enough to conduct one without the assistance of experts. Because Garvey's movement to West Africa is overtly obstructed, the Widgeons decided to leave Harlem and return to Barrington's paternal ancestral home, Macon, Georgia. I did everything in my power to dissuade them because of the multitude of Coloreds lynched in the South, domestic terrorist organizations (KKK) and last, but not least the recent Tulsa Massacre and slaughter of 1921. The South is a breeding ground where Negros' lives are continuously suppressed and forced not to embed ambitions sowing Black intellectualism, economic freedom, and overall beatitude. Barrington assured me not to worry because he has a thorough comprehension of White Supremacy. He purchased protection: a shotgun and a handgun. He is willing to die fighting; he welcomes any type of conflict from whites. He emphasizes his knowledge of former slave patrols evolving into local police departments. He has no fear of European Americans, only disdain. Barrington acquired a plethora of legal tender from the sales of his family businesses, homes in both Harlem and Georgetown. The two sisters, Ada and Anita, are well into their seventies and purchased his rowhouse in Georgetown a few years earlier. Fiona's younger sister, Saoirse (pronounced seer-sha), immigrated to the United States via Ellis Island and served as Ada and Anita's maid in Georgetown. Saoirse would inherit the property when the sisters die. Not to mention the money amassed from his Prohibition activities. Barrington laughingly says, "I have money to burn."

The Widgeons bought a three-acre plot of land intending to build their home on it in Macon, Georgia. The year 1929 proves to be a formidable year indeed. However, the Widgeons accomplished all of their goals. Their single-story brick rancher was built without delay. Barrington is so skilled with plumbing and electricity that he installed these vital facilities himself. He only hired Negro sharecroppers to help him complete his home and these men were paid quite handsomely. Fiona is still their maid in this new relocated environment. Marcus applied and was accepted at Morehouse College in Atlanta, following his mother's footsteps. The Widgeons are still conducting séances.

Macon is integral to the 'Bible Belt', but the Widgeons weren't concerned because their family's lineage profited from the spiritual practice of conducting séances. Amazingly, the Widgeons managed to bring all of their exquisite artwork and furnishings. Their chandelier is hung in the séance room, while the rest of the rooms have ceiling fans to accommodate for the smoldering heat during the summer months. They had a humongous ice box in the kitchen to store as much ice as they could muster. Plantation shutters protect the windows and allow onlookers from the outside not to be able to see inside, but the reverse is possible. I mailed them a souvenir that I bought in Paris, for them which is a doll depicting Josephine Baker. They display my gift in their sitting room on an ebony end table. Barrington built a fireplace and a carport. They had four bedrooms and two bathrooms. Indoor plumbing is so rare in the rural South, but Barrington is adept with home repairs, installations, and improvements. Barrington's father gave him detailed information about his former slave owner, so he could bond with this family regarding séances. His grandchildren are also named Widgeon. They met with Barrington's family reluctantly. Due to the sanctity of communing with the dead, these two racially diametric families stay in touch mutually with one another. Unmindful to me, Barrington is still instrumental with bootlegging via the rumrunning route to Miami. The amount of money gained from illegal booze is astronomical. He clandestinely worked in this arena successfully for over six years. He never uses bank accounts because of the exorbitant amount of income he garnered. He hides his banknotes furtively in the walls of his home, floorboards and inside the ceilings. Barrington has no respect for the USA for its deep-rooted racism. Thus, the existence of White Supremacy is his rationale for engaging in such dangerous activities.

I am ecstatic to be back at work, helping students to critically think about our world and how to apply this knowledge constructively in their lives. Scarily, Hank came to my office. I was frank with Hank.

"You are no longer my student. Thus, your visit to my office is superfluous. What do you want?"

"I read your publications, and I wanted to personally congratulate you," Hank replied with a vacuous smile.

"I appreciate your goodwill, Hank. In the future, please write a request letter to meet with me since I am no longer your professor," I implored.

"Duly noted, Professor Williams."

We exchanged our goodbyes with civility, but I could not help to wonder why Hank is so obsessed with me years after what he witnessed me do at the Krazy Kat. Although Hank tries his best to conceal his rancor for me, the look in his eyes hurl pure hatred towards me-'**If looks could kill**'. I reminisce about Pierre's wonderful apartment. In addition to his brother's polychrome photographs, he mixed those with paintings from Antoine Berjon. His proclivity for Berjon is motivated by Berjon's focus on flowers. My favorite Berjon piece is displayed boldly in his sitting room on the second floor which is entitled, 'Oil on Board Floral Still Life'. 1929 starts with a bang, but ends with an explosive burst. The St. Valentine's Day Massacre on February 14th is when seven mobsters in Chicago's North Side Mob are slaughtered in cold blood on the orders of Al

Capone. The remaining winter, spring and summer are pleasantly profitable, but autumn plummeted into an abyss of dark destitution. Barrington met once a month with Al Capone and his henchmen to delineate and stratify safe routes from New York City to Miami, Florida. The local Macon police departments are paid off to look the other way, but most of the cops are flat out afraid for their lives. Capone loves Jazz and Negro culture. He auspiciously meets Barrington in Harlem at the numerous jazz clubs there. Most Coloreds are obliged to help the Mafia with the business of bootlegging because the money is extremely profitable, and most Negros embed resentment towards the racist regime within the US government. Many of us would volunteer to undermine this country in any way that we could. Capone is mesmerized with the séance performed by the Widgeons. Barrington shared that they brought Capone's father: Gabriel from the other side. The intense elation of seeing his father again and knowing that he is swell brought tears of joy to Al's eyes. Barrington shared all of the details of Capone's séances with me. Barrington noted that Capone has the heartiest laughter; it's so contagious that everyone can't help but laugh too in his presence when he is guffawing. Capone became eternally indebted to the Widgeons for reuniting him with his beloved father. This is part of Barrington's juju…He has the power to persuade people, regardless of their race, economic status, and religion to be enthralled with him. He epitomizes charisma. People are always drawn to him, whether they hate or love him. Indifference is nonexistent when it comes to Barrington.

I will always be in love with Barrington, and I am thrilled to get an invitation to see him and his family again face-to-face. I also am curious about where Holly is because I no longer see or converse with her. But trepidation engulfs my entire being as I contemplate his close association with Al Capone and the insidious racism permeating the deep South. Barrington assures me that Capone has the best heart because he is noble and kind. Furthermore, Barrington stipulates that Capone treats his family and loyal friends with the utmost respect, steadfastness, and generosity. Overall, Capone is trustworthy, so don't believe what the Fourth estate writes on paper. Most refreshingly, Al does not have a racist bone in his body.

Masturbation on a daily basis compensates for my celibacy, and of course, a visual stimulation of Barrington is always cause for this self-induced elation. It's been this way for the past 30 years. I hope that his relationship and rapport with Marcus has improved because if it has not, I will be eternally consumed with guilt. Sometimes my penis will become so hard and erect by simply thinking about Barrington in the most innocent way. I used to get so embarrassed being in public daydreaming about him because I would worry if anyone could see the outline of my stiff, upright dick through my trousers. Not surprisingly, some sheriffs did not want to get on board with Barrington and Al. Thus, Al put a hit on them. Five sheriffs, three deputies and a dozen local policemen were beheaded, arms and legs dismembered and lastly disposed in the Ocmulgee River. This is the punishment bestowed upon any KKK member, or 'lawmen' who tries to intimidate the Widgeons. There were two cross burnings on Barrington's property and threatening notes. When the residents of Macon learned about Barrington's intimate relationship with Capone, the harassment expeditiously desisted. Not to mention, some dead and dismembered members of the KKK and local policemen in the Ocmulgee River also dissuade White racial torment towards the Widgeons. Capone does not want to hide his unscrupulous killings. Like cats, Capone wants to boast his casualties as a warning for others to comply with his bootlegging business, or they will die. These are Capone's two options without compromise. Barrington is an accomplice because he showed Capone's henchmen where these recreant miscreants live and work. Neither men fear the law or any type of authority, so eradicating any trouble is no issue for either of them. Unlike Capone, Barrington imbues so much resentment and hostility because of Garvey's failed mission transpiring from Hoover's incessant investigations, trumped charges, and illegal intrusions that he settled with relocating to Macon, Georgia, where he has ancestral roots. However, his heart is set on emigrating to Liberia, or anywhere in West Africa. Per contra, the red dirt, summer climate and vegetation in Macon are very similar to the topography and weather in West Africa. Billions of dollars are made with the illegality of selling liquor annually. Thus, high stakes are tantamount to the plethora of lives sacrificed during this era of the roaring twenties, dirty dealings, and jazz.

Barrington brought a fragrant and resplendent piece of Georgetown with him. During the Spring of 1929, he planted Yoshino Cherry Blossom tree seeds in his back yard with hopes that a sapling would appear. In a matter of months, a healthy tree sprung from the ground eagerly and ambitiously reaching for the sky. He requested when I will visit him to bring branches of cherry trees so he can graft his cherry blossom plantlet. Fiona is an excellent decoy because she would always ride along with Barrington's crew to help transport liquor to Miami, Florida. Afterall, it is a 16-hour drive to Miami. Peddling poison is a very precarious lifestyle. Yet, Barrington is always unscathed. Onlookers would see a White woman in the car and look the other way, whilst Barrington would lay flat on the seat to conceal his presence inside of the car. Fiona and Al have a close relationship and they are very fond of one another. Fiona is very visible in town, where she would report any underhanded schemes from White terrorists regarding Negroes. Her espionage is a great interception to any of the KKK's plans to harm black people. It is hilarious witnessing Fiona's Irish accent imitating white scornful Southerners.

"Will I'll be! Niggas have a White woman for a maid. What is the werld comin' toe!?" she repeated sarcastically.

Al warned Barrington to withdraw all his money from the banks due to the increasing instability of stocks. In turn, Barrington shared this same information with me. The handwriting was already on the wall when a major bank in New York City: The Bank of the United States, had to be bailed out by the Federal Reserve, in order to salvage peoples' deposits. Additionally, the American Trust and Savings Bank, known as the Indiana Bank completely foreclosed. This closure leaves many Midwesterners in limbo with mortgage liquidations and total loss of savings and deposits. I have wads of cash hidden in my home because all of my banknotes are removed from my bank. Most Negroes never used financial depositories, except wealthy ones. Al rarely uses banks because he didn't want the Feds to track his unaccounted income due to selling illegal booze. My renters always pay cash. Being bank-free is no problem for me.

My dearest Alma shuffled off her mortal coil from a heart attack. I could never replace her because she is family to me. I will have to clean and cook for myself, once and for all. I bequeathed a large sum of money to Alma's remaining family members which paid the entirety of her funeral services. It was a very simple and honorable ceremony. Her kin are very grateful for my financial gift. I have new student renters. The duration of their rental leases is usually three to six months. My finances are well intact, but again I am alone…always alone. It is mid-October and all is still with an odd chill in the air. Barrington wants to prove his loyalty to Al, so he joins Capone's men on a round trip drive to Miami. With machine guns in tow, Capone presaged Barrington about Federal informants. Barrington reminisced of this same plight when working for Garvey.

"I am very familiar with low-life government snitches," Barrington snarled.

"They are always trying to trap us," Capone stipulated.

Rumrunning through the swamps and woods of Southern Georgia and the state of Florida align with 'Strange Fruit'. They are dozens of burnt, dead, bulging-eyed, Negro men, women and children hung from a myriad of trees. Al or one of his men would always take the time to remove these dead bodies from the tree, not just for Barrington's comfort, but for the grotesqueness of the entire scene. Imagine that these people's deaths are entertainment for most White families. They even brought young children to partake in these gruesome festivities. To make the entire lynching undertaking indelible, many Whites had picnics, took family photographs, and confiscated body parts and skin for souvenirs of these tortured Coloreds. Meeting other bootleggers in Miami is exceedingly nerve-racking for Barrington. No one trusts anyone; everyone always waits with bated breath. Barrington vividly recalls three major signs of an informant: excessive nervousness, always avoiding eye contact, and their discourse is glib. Two hours seem like an eternity. Finally, the transactions are finalized and Barrington is on his way back to Macon with Fiona with their lives intact. One of the members of Al's entourage drive Barrington and Fiona, so they are unable to have intercourse with one another. However, their sexual tension between each other is dramatically exhilarating. Barrington would arouse Fiona's pussy by gently stroking her clitoris in an upward motion. He carefully orchestrated this act by concealing his hand which is inside of her panties, covered with her overcoat. Her vagina is warm, wet, and musky. He loved her vaginal scent because he would often smell his fingertips at different intervals of finger fucking her. As his thick fingers gently massages her vagina, Fiona's spine would totally relax, as her legs naturally spread wide open like the central plain in Ireland. All the while, Barrington carefully watches the driver through the mirror during his perverse act. Suddenly, a loud thud sound interrupts them. About two hours north of Miami, they get a flat tire near quick sand. The stunning gold 1929 Ford Model T begins to vanish into the muddy, bottomless pit. We have to jump out of the car as fast as we can and unload all of the alcohol. It is pitch black, with the sounds of monstrous bellowing.

"What is making that low, loud and deep grumbling sound," Barrington asks in fear.

"Male alligators in mating season – I thought you knew about dem gators?" Lenny, Capone's driver inquired in a nonchalant manner.

Barrington thought to himself, *Alligators in heat.* He almost had a heart attack. There are over 20 cases of whiskey in the one car that sank. Luckily, we are able to retrieve the precious elixir before the car disappears into the Earth without being attacked by one of those gators. Just two months ago, James Horace Alderman, an infamous Jewish gangster was hung in Fort Lauderdale for killing two coast guard officers. Dade County and South Florida in general are known for vehement violence regarding violators of Prohibition. Federal agents and rumrunners are always at odds here because booze is so plentiful. Bootlegging is the business that requires its participants to be prepared to fight and sacrifice our lives for the illegal sales and transport of alcohol. The more things change, the more they stay the same. In spite of that scary ordeal, Barrington and Fiona are still so horny that they have a threesome with Meredith as soon as they arrive home.

My mundane and monotonous life is about to get extremely eventful because the minutiae of my everyday routines no longer matter. The Fourth Estate reports on the infamous Black Tuesday, or October 29, 1929, that the U.S. stock market plummets causing America's economy to plunge into an impoverished abyss. This is such an oxymoron because the U.S. thrives rigorously during the twenties. It is surreal to actually see rich, White Anglo-Saxon Protestant men nosedive into abject poverty. Some

WASPs decide to end their lives, as opposed to facing the music and adapt to new more humbling lifestyles. The stock market crash affects global financial centers. It is as if the global economy is hit by a colossal meteorite. People endure squatters caged along the city's sidewalks during our nation's worst depression. The newly destitute are desperately trying to survive on the streets while becoming accustomed to living with no possessions, being at the mercy of Mother Nature without a roof over their heads, and begging for handouts. Homelessness continues to multiply, as does hopelessness. Not too long ago these people had homes, occupations, and dignity. Howard University closes indefinitely the week after the New York stock market crash because this pedagogical institution is federally funded. I am forever indebted to Barrington and Al for apprising me to get all of my money out of the bank. This international debacle felt similarly to the times during the Spanish Influenza because many businesses are closed and the streets are primarily vacant. Pierre called to offer me financial assistance, but I told him that I am fine. I stocked up on food items, toiletries, candles, and batteries. Looking at the window, the weather, plants and sky have not changed in any way. It is quite sunny, and the skies are clear. It's like the calm before the storm, as the adage professes. Of the three tenants, I have one sorority sister who is a member of the Alpha Kappa Alpha (AKA); she is from San Francisco. The other two renters are also from out of state. One is from Teaneck, New Jersey, while the other is a native of Toledo, Ohio. Their combined rents pay for the entirety of my mortgage. In addition to their rents, they have to buy their own food. Since times are relatively more difficult, I furnish their meals. However, the students have to prepare and cook their food. A major stipulation in my lease is that no male visitors are allowed inside of my premises unless it is a relative. The rental clause also reads, "No overnight visitors allowed."

I frequently visit Ada and Anita, who own Barrington's old rowhouse. Despite their aging, they fare well. They are still physically independent and have great use of their mental capacities. Their favorite pastime is doing crossword puzzles. Due to the chaotic economic predicament, I supply their food and other necessities needed to make their living conditions comfortable and safe. Although, many people are financially suffering, a French restaurant has a grand opening in the Adams Morgan neighborhood called, Cuisses de Grenouilles, or frog legs in English. I don't particularly care for frog legs, but I do enjoy their French onion soup, escargot, and liver pâté with cornichons. When possible, I try to treat Ada and Anita for a bite to eat at this very posh and exorbitant French eatery, Cuisses de Grenouilles. Dining here, always takes me back to Paris because of its culinary authenticity. The geriatric sisters and my university renters fill my void of loneliness. My soul was healed when I stayed with Pierre for a year in Paris. Even during the war, I always embedded an aura of dignity, freedom, and wholeness. Living and returning to the United States, the infectious dehumanization encountering Negroes on a daily basis by Whites is revolting. Despite the catastrophes occurring in the deep South, Barrington still beckons me to visit him in Macon. My main motivation is to see and hear Holly again because I missed her ethereal visions and visits. Unlike most of our fellow Americans,

Barrington and I have excellent finances. Money is not my concern. However, I am the only male guardian for my tenants and the senior sisters. The crashing stock exchange creates calamity in the streets, with rogue robbers attacking easy prey for money, food, and clothing. If I do decide to visit Barrington's family, it would be a short stay because no one will have guardianship over the new women in my life. Moreover, they would have to stay put inside of their locked residences and be vigilant to any strange sounds from the exterior. I would want them to be able to contact the police stations at any time in case of an emergency. My Kappa Alpha Psi brothers helped me devise a will. Since I have no children, I left all of my material wealth to Marcus when I die. I always try to engage with my tenants during mealtimes. They are really clean-cut young women with ambitious futures. I apprised them that I was planning a trip to Macon, and again I instructed them on what to do in my absence. Kay seems to be the leader of the pack. She is very gregarious and outgoing. She hails from Toledo. She was the lightest-skinned of the three women. Some of my fraternity brothers kept an eye on my place in my absence.

I am taking the train to Macon for a two-week vacation. I had to sit in the back (The Colored Section) because I am visibly perceived as a Negro. This is a new phenomenon for me. I have enough money to buy a first-class ticket, but my race prohibits this capability. I made sure not to make any eye-contact with the white passengers because I did not want any trouble, but I could feel their eyes glaring at me. I am like a deer caught in headlights. Perhaps, because I dress impeccably. This train ride is more frightening than fighting in World War I. The Negro restrooms are unsanitary, with urine and defecation on the walls and the floor. The food service is worse. The soup looks and tastes like brackish water and the bread is stale. I am so relieved that I brought my own treats: Reese's Peanut Butter Cups, Mother Goose and Veronese biscuits, 7-up, and popcorn. I am fortunate to have a window seat. The vistas are breathtaking from Washington, D.C. to Macon, Georgia. The Negro train porter gave me the best food wrapped in napkins: prime rib, boiled potatoes with butter, green beans, and apple pie. His purpose is to hide the excellent meal, so White patrons don't get unglued and enraged with us. The porter's name is Angus. Angus clandestinely gave me silverware to enjoy my delectable collation. I slept most of the trip, and I really needed a lot of rest. Surprisingly, I have no nightmares of being in the war. I am rested and ready to see my friend and former lover, Barrington. Marcus is away at college: Morehouse in Atlanta, living in a dormitory. Lovely Meredith greets me at the train station in her lavish, red, and new Ford Model T with leather interior.

"Are you ready for another séance?" Meredith implores.

"Yes, indeed. I want to converse with my sister Holly," I confirm.

Spending the Christmas holidays in Macon is a special treat for me. Meredith outdid herself with one of the best holiday spreads that I can recall. She cooked a honey ham, potato salad, collard greens, macaroni and cheese, sweet rolls, sweet potato and pumpkin pies. The entire setting is warm and welcoming. It feels like home to me. Like my mother, Meredith adores the smell of natural pine. Because the Widgeons do not celebrate any holidays, she hangs miniature pine wreaths around the house in order to keep it scenting festively and refreshingly. Al's wise guys returned back North two weeks ago, so I am unable to meet them. I can't say that I am too upset about that! Anyway, the séance will be tomorrow, and the Widgeons guarantee that I will be able to commune with Holly. Even though, the residence is entirely different, the layout for the séance is exactly how I remembered it. We have an even number of people attending the séance: Myself, Fiona, Meredith, and Barrington. We hold hands tightly as usual and summon Holly's name. It has been over two years since I have seen and spoken to my beautiful sister. She is youthful and wearing the same night clothes that she wore in the hospital.

"Peanut, beware of the Ides of March," she incessantly repeats.

I am clueless of what she is trying to prevent from happening. This is the gist of her entire discourse. I am so befuddled! Now, I am weary of the month of March, but it is still December. Her initial warning referred to Heather's death, so I strongly heed any of Holly's auguries. The only thing that I could envision is something positive. Hence, most residents of the District of Columbia know the peaking season of the cherry blossom trees occurs during the month of March because this is time when their blooms emblematically explode with a rose-colored brilliance. In spite of the unnerving séance, spending the Christmas holidays with the Widgeons is stupendous. We reminisce about our pasts and laugh, and laugh and laugh. Meredith sings spirituals while playing her beautiful 1925 Steinway Model B Grand black piano. Fiona, Barrington and I cheer her on with hand claps and applause. We dare not to sing in unison because Meredith has such an ethereal voice. I am proud because I maintained my celibacy in such an atmosphere of temptation. We bring the new year, 1930, in together with high hopes of positivity for the future, our economy, and the entire lives of everything on the planet. Before I left, I stand and stare at the beautiful cherry blossom tree vigorously ascending to the heavens inside of the Widgeon's backyard. Barrington also planted this cherry blossom tree for reverence of his great-grandfather's unnecessary lynching in Macon. Although, they are endemic to Japan, these stunning wonders are a triad connecting the District of Colombia, Macon, and Paris. These pinkish beauties carry losses and triumphs amalgamating into a bevy of births revealing transformation. I returned to Georgetown with bags of delectable dishes. I ate some on the train, and the remaining ones, I savor and share with my tenants. The girls fared well because they were no incidents of burglary or any other violent crime in my absence. Also, Ada and Anita did not encounter any issues.

Thanks to my fraternity brothers who kept a watchful eye on these properties, they also beckoned policemen who they knew to help prevent any possible criminal activity by frequently driving by these specific rowhouses.

The following months are quite uneventful, but my career teeters between a lot of classes per week to maybe one or two a month because of the Great Depression. March is here, and the cherry blossom trees look splendid. People are still unsure because our economy is vacillating and unpredictable. More people are in the streets begging for food. Perhaps the most disheartening observations are women and children wearing tattered clothing with dirty faces, hands, and fingernails.

To my astonishment, Hank is inside my residence! I am so floored. I don't allow anyone on my floor, and there he is. Unbeknownst to me, Hank is Kay's older brother. Johnson is such a common surname that I never gave it a second thought. He met with Kay earlier this morning at a local café for breakfast and stole her house keys right out of her purse.

"Professor Williams, you have such an expensive and elegant place for yourself," he sardonically replied.

"It was my parent's home," I stated clearly. "What is your business here?"

Without uttering a single word, Hank pulls a Tommy Gun (Thompson Submachine) from underneath his tan trench coat. I try to move crabwise to dodge his bullets. But Hank aims at my groin and shoots me. Astonishingly, I have no painful sensations. Alternatively, I am as light as a feather. I float above my physical body and I see blood gushing out of my genitals. I observe Hank drop his Tommy gun and storm out of my residence. I have no emotions – only a profound sense of peace that I never knew in life. I keep rising higher and higher. I fly slowly through my ceiling and into the clouds. The clouds transition into multicolored tulips. This spectacular place smells divine. In the near distance, I could see Holly, my parents, Max, and Mimi. Oddly, Heather is nowhere to be found. In any event, I thought to myself that this must be heaven. A bottomless and overpowering sense of joy envelops me. My dearly departed family and I traverse through a colorful tunnel where the colors make sound. We communicate with one another telepathically. Fear is a foreign concept that has no place in this newfound paradise. My precious cats and family look me in the eyes and telepathically tell me that it is not my time and that I must go back into my corporal physique. Hearing this news is the worst information I could receive. I will do anything to not go back because this realm is so euphoric and blissful. It is utterly indescribable because I have never experienced peaceful profundity like I am here in this dimension in my entire life on Earth. They smile, and I automatically travel backwards into my body. I am at Howard University hospital, and I have no memory of how I arrived here. The nurses and doctors apprise me that I was in a coma for an entire month. The Tommy gun only decimated my left testicle; however, my penis is miraculously intact. Kay turned her brother into police custody because Hank was hiding out, but he trusted Kay. The trial is daunting. Kay and I testified against Hank, but he only received five years for attempted murder. Hank never refutes his crime. Barrington wants Hank dead as a doorknob, but I persuade him not to hurt him. As knowledgeable as Barrington is regarding the afterlife, I further confirmed that it is a place of pure peace. As I told the jury and the court, I alerted Barrington that I forgive Hank. I feel blessed to be able to visit the other side and return to the living. The immense state of love that I have is so exceedingly intense. I have no fear, and it is so freeing to live this way. Doctors say that I was dead for eight minutes. The medical staff tried to revive me eight times. Before placing me inside of the body bag, they had to close my eye lids. They called the coroner and were about to put me inside of a body bag. Right before they lifted my physique,

I held my head up and opened my eyes. One of the nurses screeched as my soul reentered my physical anatomy. Now, I feel the pain! Thank goodness for morphine.

Hank hates the fact that he is gay. Thus, he will never come to terms with his sexuality. Thus, he displays displaced aggression towards me because I was able to openly express my homosexual desires. Ironically, Hank is an orthodox Pentecostal, hoping to become a minister of his own church. Kay shared this fact with me. I exude nothing but empathy for Hank; I embed no scission for him or anyone else. Thus, he is hostage inside his own psyche due to the fact that he is incapable of being who he is born to be. I certainly hope that one day homosexuals will be able to be free and not imprisoned by fear and subjugation because of the condemnation disseminated by many outsiders. My dream is that same-sex marriages will be a legal institution like heterosexual unions. Kay moved out of my home. Kay didn't have to do this, but she is so embarrassed. Kay earned her bachelor's degree in spite of her brother's infamous crime. The Washington Post printed my attempted murder, so Kay eventually moved to other pastures. I never knew where she relocated, and I think she wants to keep her new location a secret from all of the negative press. Speaking of negative news, anti-Jewish sentiments, or Antisemitism, is not just a problem in France, Spain, and Italy; but it is spreading throughout most of Europe, like the Spanish Influenza did over a decade ago. I always let Pierre and his family know that they are more than welcome to stay with me if things continue to escalate. We have no idea that in another decade, that this magnitude of hate stewing in

Europe would lead to our second world war and the infamous Holocaust.

I retired from my professorship and began a hobby of painting. Paris, Albert, and his brother: Pierre inspired me to encapsulate the world in oil paint on canvass. My hobby eventually grew into a sustainable business. I always relish putting my insignia on my artistic work because it makes me immortal. My first portrait is cherry blossom trees with a riverbank for a background, from the triad of places aptly accreted via my living experiences. My second creation is Max and Mimi. I highlighted his golden eyes and her green oculi. I deem that my greatest inspiration for painting is my near-death experience. I paint visions from my near-death journey to the other side, including sound, because I want the world to know just how beautiful everything really is and should be. I eventually reentered movie theaters. I enjoy my own company, but sometimes I could feel Heather holding my right hand or hear her faintly whispering in my ear, "I luvs you Peanut." Oddly, I never physically see Heather, I only hear, smell, and feel her. Her favorite perfume: Habanita by Molinard's scent would often gesticulate her arrival. It smells like smoked tobacco soaked in rose and orange blossom waters combined. Heather rarely smoked cigarettes, but she always wanted to be in vogue by exuding false pretenses…she was so pretentious at times, trying to mimic an avid smoker.

While painting portraits along the Potomac River, I can smell the subtle, bitter, honey-like, and intoxicating aromas of the cherry blossoms. I notice that the cherry blossoms die soon after they reach their full bloom. Thus, their authentic beauty lies in their evanescence. I accomplished one of my bucket list destinations thanks to Pierre and his brother: Albert Khan's inspiring international photographs of Tokyo, Japan. Japan reminds me so much of my beloved Paris with its red and white Tokyo Tower, which structure is a replica of the Eiffel Tower. In addition, Ueno Park is filled with a glorious display of a plethora of cherry blossom trees as far as the naked eye can see. Ueno Park also has a similarity to my hometown, The District of Columbia due to some of its park benches, tranquil energy, rivers, statues, and, of course, the Cherry Blossom Trees.

We are so much more than our limited identities. Skin tones, religions, polity, sexual orientations, economic status, genetics, and all of the other labels we doggedly depend on Earth are simply rendered useless in timeless infinity. We are eternal illuminated luminosity – beams of light balls forever entering and exiting out of consciousness. Scientifically, this makes perfect sense since we are children of stardust. Hence, every atom, molecule, and cell in our bodies emanate from supernovas and envelop the exact chemical composition of stars. 'We are one' is no cliché; alternatively, it is a scientific fact! Forgiveness is the path to freedom. I am free, happy, and at peace with myself and every being because my ego perpetually continues to transcend. The year is 1992, and I have outlived all of my friends and loved ones. I did not remarry or conceive any children. I never officially came 'Out' openly regarding my sexual orientation because I don't deem it necessary to announce my private business in the streets. Yet, I conjecture that most people observe that I am gay; I am comfortable with this actuality. Most importantly, people's opinions about me no longer phase me. Concomitantly,

Barrington surmised that Capone, Garvey and St. Clair never knew of his homosexual orientation. In any event, I have witnessed multiple revolutions and observed monumental changes within a multitude of places around the world. Three miraculous gifts of humanity that I was blessed to witness are women having the visceral right to vote, decide to choose to have legalized abortions, and I beheld human beings walk on the moon. I stand corrected because the moon landing is more of a cosmic phenomenon. Yet, two of the worst global cataclysms occurred during World War II: The Jewish Holocaust and the nuclear bombing of Hiroshima and Nagasaki in Japan. These two particular events revealed our vulnerable mortality. Pierre and I could never envision that anti-Semitism and xenophobia, via fascism in Europe, would ever escalate to the levels of global genocide and grisliness that lead and endured into World War II. Lamentably, Albert informed me that Pierre was wrested to the infamous concentration camp: Auschwitz. I loved Pierre like a brother; he was my true platonic friend. Since his arrival to Auschwitz, neither one of us heard from him again. Hence, we only assumed the worst. To add insult to injury, all of his personal belongings were confiscated when Nazis ransacked his home. His jewelry, paintings, clothing, and monetary bills had a network of over one million dollars. With the advent of the atom bomb, at this precise moment, the tangibility of having the power to end everything as we know it on planet Earth via violence is an ego booster, yet quite terrifying.

I learned how to drive automatic cars, cook with microwave ovens, operate computer word processors, relax when flying on commercial airplanes, listen to the

Walkman, view video home system (VHS) players and tapes, maneuver automated teller machines (ATM), and facsimile (fax) gadgets. The wonders of exponential technological growth never cease to amaze me. My stroke finally got the best of me, as I physically appear lifeless in palliative care. The finishing image I have is Barrington's youthful face of 15 years of age, holding my hand and sitting alongside my deathbed. Barrington transitioned into the other dimension 30 years prior on this exact date of a heart attack. His passing was one of the hardest losses that I ever endured! Barrington squeezes my fingers ever so tightly to make sure that I know he is really here instead of me confusing this wonder as a figment of my imagination, welcoming me before I undertake my second transitioning. Out of nowhere, concomitantly, Mimi and Max bounce on the foot of my bed, purring ever so loudly, while clawing into the blanket. Max walks onto my upper torso, neck, then nose because he wants to give me a kiss. He completes his mission by licking my face. The final sound I hear emanates from the alarm beeping from the ventilator machine. 'Sakura' is my last verbiage taken along with my vanishing breath, as a single tear of joy runs down my left visage. The beautiful hospice nurse quietly smiles at me while she fades into the distance. The fiat of our universe and cosmos is pure consciousness because we are intrinsically one with everything. At the ripe age of 103, I immerse into a semi-unfamiliar dimension, which is liken to a fast-moving wormhole delivering beings via a portal of brilliant vocalized light awaiting us at the end only to begin again.